Dr. Grady Hunter has a vampire infestation on his hands in the town of Shady Pines, but he's been deserted by those best suited to help. After enlisting Chris Reed, a techno-mage, they find the vampires might only be the tip of a deadly iceberg.

Returning home from his dream travels, Ethan Roam is eager to experiment with his newly discovered powers. But Ethan isn't the only familiar arrival in Grady's life. As more reminders of his dark past crop up, Grady and Ethan are swept up in a mystery of cosmic proportions.

Grady must fight to keep an ever-evolving Ethan on his side while being challenged by the ghosts of his past.

HUNTER

Roam, Book Two

Dez Schwartz

A NineStar Press Publication

Published by NineStar Press
P.O. Box 91792,
Albuquerque, New Mexico, 87199 USA.
www.ninestarpress.com

Hunter

Printed in the USA
First Edition
April, 2019

Print ISBN: 978-1-950412-55-6

Also available in eBook, ISBN: 978-1-950412-40-2

Warning: This book contains sexual, which may only be suitable for mature readers.

With eternal gratitude and love to Nick and Alyse. Special thanks to mom and dad, Jenn, Gaby, and all the readers who have made it possible for me to tell my stories. I dedicate this book to my tribe: the misfit dreamers.

"A dreamer is one who can only find his way by moonlight, and his punishment is that he sees the dawn before the rest of the world."

~ Oscar Wilde ~

One: Vampires. Why Did It Have To Be Vampires?

THE OLD PARK in Shady Pines was the stuff of nightmares. Or so it would seem to anyone who happened upon the derelict area after the sun set. In actuality, it was simply a park. Located across from the oldest district in the small Texas city of Shady Pines and near the edge of a small forest encompassing the town, the park was extremely rundown and typically abandoned during the daytime. A snapshot of times past, the neglected playground had standard metal slides and jungle gyms, before modern worries of bruises, broken bones, and burns on hot afternoons. Like most cities, Shady Pines had since created newer and safer places for families to gather. And so, the old park had fallen to ruin but still remained hopeful its ghosts would return to play again.

As it happened, quite a few creatures loved to play there, but they were rarely of the human set. Part of what made the place so eerie was park's location. Once sunset arrived, a thick fog would roll in from the marshes in the woods and overtake the area. If one were to stand there, as Dr. Grady Hunter was doing now, the murky haze would only rise to roughly one's waist depending on their height. The moon would hang bright and looming overhead, as it also was now, to cast shadows all around.

And a breeze would cause swings to sway, and the paint chipped merry-go-round to spin ever so slightly, as was also happening now. At least, one would hope the movement was due to the breeze. Unless, of course, the person *was* Dr. Grady Hunter and was hoping for something else.

"Any signs of movement? Blast this fog!" Grady, a semi-former monster hunter and more recently self-appointed alternative healer of supernaturals, whispered into the small microphone on the headset he was wearing. His British accent was always strongest when he was frustrated. The park wasn't his first choice of venue to lure vampires, but any abandoned buildings or dark alleys would provide them too much of an advantage and surely seem like a setup. They would definitely be suspicious. He supposed they *should* be suspicious of a man in his late thirties strolling through the old park at night alone but, as the case happened, they appeared to find that behavior completely normal.

"Nada. And don't worry about the fog. The visuals I'm pulling from my cameras penetrate right through it." A casually confident, and extremely American in contrast, male voice replied back from the other side of the communication device between sounds of chewing.

"Are you eating right now? We're working!" Grady admonished, still in a whisper as he slowly strolled through the park with his hand hovering by his waist. He had a number of weapons at the ready beneath his long brown coat in case he was successful in finding what he was looking for.

"Please, I'm the king of multitasking. Besides, it's past my dinnertime and I can't refuse a sushi place if I pass one," the voice responded. Grady could tell the man on the other side, Chris Reed, was smiling. Then, he became urgent. "Ahab, you've got a white whale at ten o'clock."

"That's not my code name. We don't have code names. Don't make things up on the spot. It's distracting," Grady griped but whipped around to face whatever was heading his way.

"If we did, though, I think I'd want to be Zaphod," Chris replied, obviously slurping a drink. "Your target is hovering by the slide. Not the loopy one. The tall straight one. I fell off a slide once when I was a kid. I was pretending to be Indiana Jones. Broke my wrist. Great summer."

"Your lifelong aspiration to be fictional characters is both charming and annoying. Going silent now," Grady replied as he stalked slowly in the direction of the slide. He reached inside his jacket for a stake. He saw a figure's shadow wavering across the top of the fog. It definitely appeared human, which most likely meant it was a vampire. He tried to keep his weapon concealed beneath the haze and pretended he was simply walking in the same direction, unaware of the creature's presence.

"Whip out the big boy! It's an ambush from behind!" Chris shouted in his ear. Unable to keep from chuckling, he added, "That didn't come out how I meant. But seriously, you're under attack. "

Grady immediately switched to a revolving handheld crossbow, which was loaded with a round of stakes, should a situation such as this ever arise. He spun on his heel in time to see four vampires running full speed in his direction. He shot one down but then had to momentarily turn his attention back to the first vampire, who had taken the opportunity to pounce on him.

Grady wrestled free of his grip and knocked him onto the slide where he toppled over the edge and onto the ground.

"Yeah, pretty much how I broke my wrist," Chris commented.

"Oh, do shut up!" Grady shouted back in the mic. The outburst caused some mild confusion for the vampires as none of them had been speaking, but it didn't deter them from continuing their attack.

Two of the vampires lifted Grady and slammed him into the ground on his back, knocking the wind out of him. He felt a cracking pain he didn't have time to assess, as one of the vampires straddled his chest and went fangs-first for his neck. He managed to pull the revolver up to the creature's chest and let loose a stake right before he was torn into. He rolled free, still with three vampires to face and precisely three stakes left in his crossbow.

"This is exciting. You're doing a great job, boss!" Chris complimented.

"Not! Helpful!" Grady panted as he attempted to catch his breath. He didn't get much of a break as another vampire grabbed him by the shoulder and jerked his arm backward, trying to rip the crossbow from his grasp. Grady shouted in response to the wrenching pain.

"Keep him there!" Chris commanded. "I can get a shot in. He's right in the line of fire."

"I'm not the one in control at the moment, thank you!" Grady grieved between gritted teeth as he tried to maintain control of the weapon against the thrashing pull of the vampire. Thankfully, the vampire on the other side of the slide was only now running over to try to help his cohort, and the third had opted to watch the scene rather than participate.

A wild shot seemed to fly in out of nowhere. Grady knew the attack came from one of the cameras they had placed around the park for their mission. Attached to the bottom of each supernatural night vision camera was a small loaded device that would shoot a stake with bullet-like precision when activated. It was one of the many weapons they'd had to develop and utilize in the past few months as the vampire infestation in Shady Pines had progressively gotten worse and Grady found himself without much help in dealing with the problem.

Ethan Roam, his new partner in both work and life—who happened to be a sandman, was still away dream traveling. Benny, weredog and roommate, was living the high life as a spoiled Chihuahua fifty percent of the time, rendering him practically ineffective. Vivian Edwards, a highly skilled witch and his former secretary, refused to speak to him or respond to any of his messages. Ethan's mother, Karen Roam, and their mutual friend, Dr. Arthur Ellis, were eager to help. However, while they were fine comrades in research, they were useless in the field. Grady had no choice but to call upon an old acquaintance to help with the crisis. Chris Reed, a rogue hunter and techno-mage. Thankfully, Chris was more than capable and equally enthusiastic at the prospect. He enjoyed inventing new ways to destroy and capture supernatural creatures, and he'd decided working with Grady was a fantastic way to demo his creations. Unfortunately, even with Chris's handiwork and help, they hadn't made much of a dent in the vampire population, which was rapidly growing and terrorizing the citizens (and other paranormals) who generally enjoyed a night out from time to time.

The shot hit the vampire perfectly, and Grady fell forward onto his knees, free of the monster's grasp. This, however, caused the crossbow to fly free from the ended struggle and fall into the fog. Grady couldn't see where the weapon landed and began swearing. Knowing he had only moments, he reached back into his jacket and produced two khukuri knives. He stood quickly, ready to face the vampire who had been standing by watching, but was surprised to find he'd disappeared.

"Bugger! One escaped. Did you see where he went?" Grady asked into the mic as he rounded on the last vampire, already furiously leaping toward him.

"Dammit! No. I'm sorry," Chris replied. "I had my eye on my shot."

Grady pulled up the khukuri knives on either side of the vampire's throat as the creature attempted to attack him. The vampire's eyes grew wide in surprise, realizing he was about to be beheaded. He met Grady's gaze in a pleading manner. Grady hated when they did that. It made him think of Dacey Sinnett, the only vampire he'd ever call a friend, and he suddenly felt sick to his stomach. Grady did his best to keep his resolve.

"Tell me who is leading you, or I will end you right now!" Grady demanded, his expression ferociously serious.

"You'll do it anyway," the vampire spat back.

Grady shoved his weight forward and slammed him up against the slide, blades tightly gripped around the vampire's neck.

"Your cooperation may convince me otherwise. Now answer the question!" he commanded again.

"You're great at playing bad cop, Grady," Chris interjected in his ear. Once again, he practically heard him grinning. Grady wished he could rip his headset off but right now his hands were full.

"I don't know his name," the vampire played along. "He showed up out of nowhere a few months ago. Started making promises and threats; demanding that we help him."

"Help him with what?" Grady seized the opportunity to gather much-needed information. "And is he a vampire? A human? Something else?"

"He wants us to tear this pathetic town to pieces until we find—" The vampire's answer was forever halted as he was hit expertly with a stake.

"Dammit! Chris, was that you?" Grady yelled angrily.

"No!" Chris was defensive. Grady stood, with no vampire left to interrogate, and looked around. He saw the source at the same time Chris must have on the cameras.

"Guess he found your crossbow," Chris sighed limply as the last vampire, the one who had gone missing, ran off into the night after killing their only chance at finding some answers.

Grady kicked the slide in frustration which caused a metallic gong to echo around the now empty park. They weren't any closer to dealing with the problem or having any real answers.

"Sorry tonight was a bust, man," Chris consoled.

"Same story, different night," Grady sighed. He brushed off as much dirt and grass from his jacket and pants as possible and attempted to calm his frustrations.

"Don't worry, tiger. We'll get them one of these days." Chris was already back to his upbeat self. "If it's any consolation, you looked like a total badass. I have to admit, watching you fight has to be my second favorite thing about this gig."

"Oh, really? And what's the first?" Grady smirked. Chris didn't let anyone feel down for too long.

"The inevitable moments where I get to save your ass, of course," Chris chimed.

"Prat." Grady rolled his eyes but smiled anyway as he headed back through the park toward his old Jaguar.

"Twat," Chris responded without missing a beat. Grady chuckled. If nothing else, at least having Chris around kept up morale.

"Go ahead and take the rest of the night off," Grady said, getting into his vehicle. He glanced back at the park once more, in case he missed something, but the area remained quiet and empty. "I suppose Benny already went home?"

"Yeah, he left a while back. He said watching would make him nervous. And to be honest, I'm not much of a fan of small yapping dogs," Chris replied. Grady heard him shutting off various equipment in the background.

"All right. See you tomorrow, then." Grady turned off the headset and tossed the device into the passenger seat. He leaned back into the headrest and closed his eyes, inhaling deeply and slowly letting his breath back out.

"*Find.* What could they possibly want to find so badly in Shady Pines?" Grady asked himself aloud as he recalled what the vampire tried to tell him. The pit of his stomach tightened and his heart grew heavy because he had a pretty good idea of what, or whom, that might be.

He brought the car to life and drove straight home, feeling the need to be at Ethan's sleeping side.

A LITTLE BROWN yapping Chihuahua was precisely what greeted him as he stepped into the foyer of his large gray two-story Victorian manor. Every light in the house appeared to be on and the various array of Victorian and Georgian furniture, décor, and antiques gave the home a warm, glowing ambiance.

Benny, the "werehuahua" as everyone semi-jokingly referred to him, was bouncing on his hind legs and wagging his tail fervently. Grady noticed his housekeeper, a ghost named Agatha, who usually came to greet him, was absent.

Benny latched his teeth into the leg of Grady's trousers and started tugging.

"Benny!" Grady scolded gently. "What on earth has gotten into you? I'm rather fond of these pants. They're Cordings, I'll have you know."

Benny let go of his pant leg and dashed across the hallway toward the main receiving room in an excited hurry.

"You can teach him to sit, fetch, and turn into a human boy, but you can't teach him manners," Grady grumbled, hanging up his coat and following the little dog's steps.

He immediately stopped short in the doorway of the room. Anything and everything else that had happened that night was quickly forgotten. For there, sitting in the two wingback chairs by his fireplace, were the last two men he expected to ever see together and they were both staring at him expectantly.

Agatha, the resident housekeeping ghost, was floating around diligently serving tea. Karen Roam, Ethan's incredibly supportive mother, was seated on the green lounge chair across from the visitors as she accepted a drink. Benny was running around in excited circles between the legs of the chairs.

Grady wasn't aware he'd stopped breathing momentarily, because staring back at him was not only his lover, Ethan Roam, wide awake with vibrant, otherworldy eyes but also a much older man he thought he'd never see again for the rest of his life.

Edwin Quinn. His father.

Two: Alexander Quinn

GRADY RELISHED THE comforting cheerfulness breaking free within him as he embraced Ethan Roam. He pressed his cheek into the side of Ethan's face, both in an effort to be closer to him, and also to hide his overly joyful expression. There were onlookers present, after all, and he wasn't used to having an audience for sentimentality. He still gripped him tightly, however, and was relieved Ethan was equally enthusiastic to see him.

Grady worried Ethan would see the multiverse in all of its glory and realize how insignificant Grady actually was. Thank heavens he didn't seem to feel that way in the slightest. When he first entered the room, Ethan looked at Grady as if nothing else in existence could ever match his magnificence. If their embrace lasted forever, Grady would have been perfectly happy.

Eventually, they had to pull back, though, and Grady considered him with content adoration. "It's so very good to have you back."

"It's good to be back." Ethan grinned. He bit down awkwardly on his lower lip, ran his fingers through his own mussy black hair, and shifted his weight to one foot. Grady knew his mannerisms well enough to know his fidgeting was a sign of his self-consciousness. He noticed Ethan's glance dart momentarily to the older man, Edwin Quinn, who was watching them with all manner of interest and uncomfortable confusion. Grady placed a comforting hand on Ethan's shoulder to indicate he shouldn't worry about their unexpected guest.

"I have so much to tell you. But—" Ethan glanced to Edwin again. "—it can wait. You have a more important conversation first."

"Nothing is more important to me than you," Grady stated, straightening his shoulders. He purposefully positioned himself to face Ethan as he spoke; turning his back to everyone else.

"Same," Ethan offered Grady with a warm smile. "But it's okay. Really. Mom said she wanted to cook me a 'welcome back' dinner. We'll be in the kitchen." He patted Grady lightly on the shoulder. Ethan signaled to his mother, and she politely set down her teacup and gracefully crossed the room toward them.

"Don't worry." She smiled warmly to Grady, her kind blue eyes twinkling. "I won't let him take off again before you two get a real chance to talk."

Grady offered them a small nod of reluctant agreement, and they quietly let themselves out of the room. Agatha quickly floated out ahead of them with clear intent of supervising their use of her kitchen.

"C'mon, Benny. You too," Ethan's voice called back to the little brown Chihuahua. The tiny dog barked excitedly at the prospect of food and scampered out after them.

Grady stood with his back turned to his father. He had absolutely no desire to have any conversation with him. Hence his leaving home and never returning.

Unfortunately, he knew he had to face him now, so he set his jaw and gathered his resolve.

"Well, one thing certainly hasn't changed," Grady remarked as he turned around and strode over to the empty wingback chair next to the fireplace, across from where his father was seated. "Your timing is still absolutely terrible."

"Yes." Edwin graciously allowed the insult. "I seem to have interrupted a happy return. I do apologize for that. But I don't apologize for showing up. "

"Obviously," Grady said begrudgingly. He looked at his oxfords and frowned at the muck the soles had acquired at the park. He was doing his best to avoid eye contact. It was odd. After all these years and everything he'd experienced, he still felt like a child in the presence of his father.

Edwin Quinn was nearing seventy, but one might never guess as much. He looked much younger and was still very full of life due to his good health and athletic nature. He was tall like Grady, had the same gold-flecked blue-green eyes, and matching high cheekbones; genetic traits were clearly strong in the line of Quinn men. The only difference was Edwin's features were now lined with the wrinkles and white hairs of age and worry. His eyesight also wasn't what it used to be as he now donned a pair of stylish white-rimmed glasses which made it apparent Grady had inherited his preference for dapper high-end fashion as well.

"I don't understand, Alexander," Edwin sighed with frustration. He leaned forward in his chair, practically pleading for the truth. "Why do you treat me as though I've done something wrong? You disappeared without a word! I understand the circumstances were... But did your mother and I really deserve to be cut off from you? We could have helped you!"

"No, you could not have!" Grady shot back, looking up into the face of the man he hadn't seen in almost two decades. The man everyone had expected him to grow up to be exactly like. The man he almost became. He couldn't picture himself being further from that person than he was now.

"And don't call me Alexander," Grady corrected, bringing his voice back to a normal pitch. "I'm Dr. Grady Hunter now. Alexander Quinn is dead. He died from a tragic suicide due to grief and heartbreak. You can take that story back to the Cotswolds if they're still keen on finding out what happened to me."

Grady sank into his chair and turned his gaze upon the flickering flames of the fire beside them. He'd lost himself in thought to their dancing artistry many times. Some people imagined shapes in clouds, but he rewrote history in flames.

The last thing he wanted on the night Ethan finally returned was to have his past life revisited. But here it was. His memories and pain over Ava's gruesome murder came flooding back. He had hoped destroying the werewolf who was responsible would have quelled his personal torture and anger at the injustice of it all, but especially now, he realized those feelings would never go away. They could only be compartmentalized, kept dormant, and locked away. This conversation wasn't going to allow that.

"I can't tell your mother such a thing," Edwin argued at Grady's attempted dismissal. "She'd be devastated. More so than she is already over you leaving."

"Then make up your own tale. As long as it doesn't lead anyone else from my past to my doorstep, I honestly don't care what you decide to tell people," Grady responded coldly. After a silent moment of clashing wills, he spoke again. His tone was less harsh now, "How is Mother?"

"Other than missing you and her perpetual anxiety over my traveling, she's doing very well. Age hasn't slowed her one bit." Edwin smiled at him kindly. Despite Grady's annoyed countenance, it was obvious he was glad to see his son alive and well.

"You appear to be doing quite well yourself in this new life," he added as he scanned the room full of expensive furniture and antiquities.

"I manage," Grady offered simply. He pinched his thumb and index finger on the bridge of his nose, squeezing his eyes shut, as he attempted to compose himself. Shutting out the vivid, horrific recollections of seeing Ava's mangled body and also the immense love he'd felt for her in his youth before her death by Marius, the werewolf, was proving difficult. Every time his father spoke, Grady felt he was being involuntarily transported back in time. To a time when Ava was alive and smiling up at him, giggling, as they kissed in the cool green grass after a picnic lunch. He still remembered the way the sunlight caught the strawberry strands of hair, which blew and spun across her face in the breeze, like glistening strands of fresh golden honey. How soft the pale skin of her shoulders felt when he slipped off the straps of her sundress. He could still feel the warm brush of her lips against his and the satisfying taste of her moist cherry lip gloss as he lost himself in her embrace.

And then, for the millionth time, he remembered she was dead, and he would never hear her laugh again or receive her sweet and gentle kisses. The warm memories morphed to dark ash, like kindling in the fireplace.

Those dark thoughts brought on memories of others who had touched his life since then. Of Marguerite Blackwood, corrupted and possibly insane. And Dacey

Sinnett, who had been full of endless surprises but never willingly accountable for anything. Their imperfections had given him a false sense of security. The idea that he couldn't be hurt by someone he didn't love. A lie. It still hurt. They, too, were dead and gone now.

And now he had Ethan, an unpredicted risk of the heart. Someone he loved more than anyone else he'd ever known, and he'd become consumed with fear of ever losing him. A pain he could never endure. One he knew would be the end of him. Every day he waited in the wings of his own tragic opera to find out how cruel the Fates could truly be. His life had become one long-held breath.

Watching the flames no longer helped. They were mocking him. How dare they continue to burn so brightly when everyone he'd ever cared for kept having their own light taken away and those who lived were always on the brink of darkness.

"You look like you need a drink." Edwin's concerned voice broke through his thoughts.

Grady snorted a short laugh and sighed. The mundaneness of the sentiment broke the tension, and he gave his father his attention in full.

"Well, you're right about that," Grady agreed. He forced himself out of his despair, and his chair, and strode to the small bar area to the right. He popped open the wooden cabinet doors and grabbed two tumblers before pouring them both a glass of bourbon. He always had the spirit on hand. Dacey apparently had an endless supply and would gift the drink to everyone quite frequently since, being a vampire, he didn't partake. The method did win a vast array of fast friends, however, and Grady supposed that was his plan all along.

"I know it must be difficult to see me, and I won't ask for details," Edwin said, accepting the drink Grady offered. "But...you know what they say about you?"

"That I'm a serial killer?" Grady guessed. He took a sip of the whiskey and sat again. "Yes. Rather hard to miss that slight against my character."

"I don't believe it, of course," Edwin reassured him. However, he did look rather grim.

"So why bring it up?" Grady wondered. He eyed his father with mild suspicion.

"Well, that wasn't exactly the rumor I was referring to," Edwin admitted. His eyes were now dancing with a curiosity Grady couldn't recall ever seeing in them; in turn, this roused Grady's own curiosity.

"Oh? Then what else must I know concerning my reputation?" Grady asked. He took another sip of his drink to steady his nerves.

"I've seen things," Edwin started. And then stopped. He appeared unable to find the right words but, after a brief moment, he continued. "While tracking you, I came across a number of...well, *odd* people. To shorten the story... I'm inclined to believe in a lot of things I wouldn't have before. Your ghost maid, for one, provides a great example."

Grady offered a small smile of amusement as he finished his drink.

"There are some back home who think you may, in fact, be a werewolf. They believe that's why you fled. Your mother, of course, takes great offense at all accusations," he revealed.

"Mother was always fantastic at being offended," Grady said. "I find it rather offensive myself, honestly, that there are those willing to believe in such a creature's existence while simultaneously holding such a low opinion of me that they would still prefer to place the blame on my shoulders."

"Was there really a werewolf?" Edwin had obviously been dying to ask the question for a number of years.

"Yes," Grady confirmed, setting his empty glass on the side table. "Though, to the disappointment of the eccentrics and trolls of the Cotswolds, it wasn't me."

"There are trolls in the Cotswolds too?" Edwin's brows rose.

"No. At least not any of the supernatural variety," Grady clarified.

Edwin simply nodded; although, he appeared immensely relieved. The conversation seemed to find a dead end at this juncture.

"It's rather late," Grady pointed out.

"Yes," Edwin agreed. "I'm not used to being up all hours of the night like you young ones. I should be going."

"Nonsense. I have plenty of open rooms. You're welcome to stay here," Grady offered, ever the gentleman.

"I appreciate that. Very much," Edwin said genuinely. "But I'd be imposing too much. I have a hotel room. I'll be fine there. "

"No. You won't," Grady revealed. "Not to put too fine a point on the matter, but we have an ordeal with a group of vampires at present. If you've followed me here, then I must take the precautionary assumption someone else may have followed *you*. For your safety and mine, I'd prefer you remain under my watch while you're in Shady Pines. Karen is here for similar reasons. Benny can help you bring your things over tomorrow."

"Benny?" Edwin appeared, understandably, confused. "The dog?"

"I'm afraid my life is going to be quite a culture shock for you," Grady mused.

"Yes. It does seem rather American," Edwin agreed.

Grady finally offered an authentic smile, which caused his father to return the same.

"I'm not here to damage your new life," Edwin reassured. "I don't expect you to come home or anything of the sort. Maybe I'd like if you called your mother, but I won't press the issue. I just want to get to know my son again."

"I understand. But I'm afraid all I have to offer is the chance for you to get to know Grady Hunter," Grady replied. "There's no going back for me at any rate."

"That's enough for me, Grady." Edwin smiled kindly. "If anyone ever asks, Dr. Grady Hunter is simply a friend of the family. No relation."

"Thank you," Grady stated appreciatively. The fire now felt friendly again, offering a sense of welcoming to his home. He rang a small bell on the side table, and Agatha swept into the room through the wall.

"Agatha, would you please see that Mr. Quinn gets settled in his room? Preferably, one at the far end on the upstairs hall," Grady advised. He didn't mind having his father stay there, but he certainly wanted to keep his distance and have his privacy. Ethan was back now, after all.

The ghost maid nodded and disappeared to get everything in order.

"She'll return to fetch you shortly," Grady explained. Even though Edwin said he'd seen a number of odd things he still looked...well...as though he'd seen a ghost.

"I don't mean to pry too much," Edwin said, still staring at the space Agatha had previously occupied.

Eventually, he turned back to Grady, "But...what is the situation with the boy?"

Grady had been wondering how long it would take for this interrogation to arise. He had hoped he'd be able to put it off awhile longer.

"He's not a boy. He's an adult," Grady elucidated. He felt heat sweeping across his cheeks, which was a rare occurrence. Not many things made Grady blush. The subject of his intimacy with Ethan, however, was one of them.

"Eighteen? Nineteen?" Edwin, much to Grady's dismay and umbrage, actually ventured to guess.

"He's twenty. What of him?" Grady tried not to let his voice give anything away, but he came across too purposefully.

"So, it's like *that* then?" Edwin asked; though, clearly, he had pieced it together on his own. "I had no idea you... Well, you never indicated—"

"There's quite a lot you don't know. Add it to the list of rumors. I understand it's rather long," Grady interrupted. He wondered what was taking Agatha so long. "I'm glad to welcome you into my home, but you'll do best to leave your judgment at the door."

"Oh, I'm not judging," Edwin clarified. "Not in the way you think, at any rate. Or at all, really. It's quite an age difference—seventeen years. Don't you think?"

"If age gaps bother you, then I'd better not mention my last boyfriend," Grady retorted. He was, of course, speaking of the vampire, Dacey, who had been at least a hundred years his elder.

His quick wit brought him an unexpected sense of closure. This was the first time he'd ever referred to Dacey as his "boyfriend." He'd never considered him as such when they were together. In fact, he thought he'd felt nothing positive toward him during that time. But now, in retrospect, he realized that was precisely what he'd been, and he felt a sense of pride—all things considered. He hadn't given the vampire an ounce of respect when he was around, but from now on, he made a mental note to do his best to honor his memory.

"Oh, my. Very American, indeed," Edwin offered his own humor in return, which lightened Grady's mood on the subject.

Agatha suddenly appeared again, to Grady's relief, and gestured for Edwin to follow her to his room. Before he left, Edwin shook Grady's hand as an unspoken understanding of acceptance passed between them.

"Good night, Dr. Hunter." Edwin smiled kindly.

"Good night, Mr. Quinn. We'll catch up more tomorrow," Grady reassured as he saw him out of the room.

Once Edwin had disappeared upstairs with Agatha, Grady quickly made his way to the kitchen to properly welcome home the one person, with whom he had actually wanted a reunion.

Three: In Flux

KAREN ROAM AND Benny, the werehuahua, politely ducked out of the kitchen as soon as Grady appeared. There would be plenty of time to catch up later, and he was certain they knew they'd be in the way of the reunited lovers.

"That's an odd development," Ethan Roam mused after swallowing a bite of his cheeseburger. He gestured in the direction of his mother's departing figure as he took a sip of iced tea and raised his eyebrows inquisitively at Grady.

Grady glanced over his shoulder with mild confusion until the meaning of the remark fully registered. He crossed his arms behind his back and tilted his head to the side in consideration as he turned his attention back to Ethan.

"Her living here temporarily? I suppose. But I felt the precaution necessary," he replied, striding over to take a seat on one of the wooden stools, which surrounded the kitchen island, where Ethan had decided to take his dinner.

"Due to the vampire infestation?" Ethan guessed, dipping a French fry into a massive helping of ketchup. "She filled me in on some of the stuff I've missed. I'm gone for three months and all hell breaks loose. "

"You think you're joking, but that's rather an apt assessment." Despite the subject, Grady lit up. He was full of adoration, relief, and longing as he finally had the man he loved awake and by his side again.

Ethan grinned in return but continued to eat his dinner.

"Of all the choices for a homecoming—burgers and fries?" Grady teasingly admonished his taste.

"I haven't had a decent meal in ages, let alone anything I'd call comfort food. There was only one thing I missed almost as much as you while I was gone," Ethan admitted. "Ketchup. Man, did I miss ketchup! I never fully appreciated it before, but after traveling the multiverse without it, I will *never* make that mistake again. I was thinking I should always pack a travel bag and make sure it's fully stocked with those annoying little packets that never tear open properly."

Ethan mimed opening a packet in the air. Obviously, trying to be cute, the attempt was working.

"And so we earthlings shall make our mark across the multiverse in the form of condiment litter. Why am I not surprised?" Grady jested. "You did it then? You were able to escape the Dream World and travel farther? On your own?" He was impressed, but his tone was laden with concern.

"Well, not on my own. Not entirely," Ethan admitted, staring at his food. "Kit helped me."

"The fox girl. The kitsune? She traveled with you?" Grady encouraged, interested to know more. He'd leaned his elbow on the table and was resting his head casually on his fist, but his attention was fixed anxiously on Ethan.

"Not exactly." Ethan met his gaze. He was practically brimming with excitement now. "We figured out a way to communicate outside the Dream World. Well, she already knew how to. It was something she and my dad used to do. Anyway, she taught me. Psychic linking. It was like I always had someone there, even when I didn't."

"Implying there were times when you did." Grady scrutinized the statement with overt curiosity.

"The multiverse is far from empty of life, Grady. That many planes of existence? Each universe in every dimension is piggybacking on one another infinitely. All blissfully unaware of each other in their own little bubbles. Well, most of them are unaware. Life? There's plenty of life. The multiverse is thriving with it," Ethan revealed. He was beaming, obviously pleased to divulge his knowledge of universal secrets.

"We're talking about alien life? Interdimensional travel? You've achieved these things and seen these things." Grady's statement was more of him trying to persuade himself those things were true and he wasn't dreaming.

"Yes and yes." Ethan smiled broadly once more. Grady noticed his eyes still sparkled with vibrant youth, but they were now also filled with the subtle depth of wisdom. He didn't doubt he was quite possibly the most enlightened man on Earth now. How could anyone have possibly seen more or known more?

"And here I was thinking vampires were the worst of my problems. My boyfriend has been off canoodling with aliens. How very James T. Kirk of you," Grady teased with a playful smirk.

He definitely didn't want Ethan thinking he wasn't thrilled for his adventures, but the truth was the idea was making him a bit insecure. Grady wasn't accustomed to being the self-conscious one in a relationship. He wasn't much accustomed to relationships at all, for that matter. Not ones he took seriously, anyway. He hardly imagined being the jealous type either, but here he was. He should be asking about scientific implications, telepathic and psychic possibilities, interdimensional portals, the goddamn topography of undiscovered planets in unknown galaxies for fuck's sake—but no. No. He was caught up in imagining Ethan writhing around with nude muscular plant men who had four arms, and who knows how many multiples of other generously sized appendages?

Ethan laughed. "Not quite. Not at all, actually. You know, the truth is that even when I was visiting a vastly populated place, I always felt alone. That's why I came back. One major reason, anyway. I realized something very important."

"Oh?" Grady wasn't about to give any more of his thoughts away.

"None of it matters if you're not there to see it with me," Ethan said. He took Grady's hand in his and squeezed tightly.

"I know it's possible," Ethan continued. "I want to take you with me next time. The problem is...it's kind of against mandated laws. The whole thing is complicated and, like most politics, kind of messy and completely obtuse. And to be honest, I don't even know if anyone enforces those rules anymore. They may all have died off. The kitsunes aren't very helpful in sorting out pertinent information or keeping up with current events and interdimensional history if it doesn't directly concern them. The other problem is I have no idea how to actually, physically, do it. I know my dad used to transport supernaturals all the time. And I accidentally brought Marius here. There's got to be an easy way. My dad figured it out. I've tried everything I could think of, but I can't make it happen."

Grady clasped his hands tightly around Ethan's, both to slow the rapid-fire explanation and to offer moral support. He wanted to cry and praise him for being the perfect sweet soul he was, but his personality was too reserved for such antics, so instead, he stared into his eyes purposefully and extended a gentle kiss.

They'd both longed for each other's touch equally. The tender kiss of gratitude quickly became a lustful embrace of passion. Once again, Grady thought if he weren't so reserved, he'd knock the dishes off the island and have his way with Ethan right then and there. *Imagine how upset Agatha would be!* The thought made Grady chuckle and he pulled back from the kiss.

"Perhaps we should take this reunion upstairs?" he offered with a lascivious grin.

Ethan rolled his eyes and teased, "Gee, is that such a good idea with my *mom* up there? I feel like I'm in high school all over again."

"I thought you told me you were never with anyone else." Grady pointed out in playful mockery.

"Okay. Let me amend that statement. What I *imagine* high school might have been like were I not a total loser," Ethan remarked as he reached forward to brush back a couple of curls that had sprung loose from Grady's perfectly styled coif.

"Don't insult the man I love," Grady countered, still smiling. "At any rate, your mother is far from our rooms and perfectly aware of the passions of men. If she's accepted me into your life to this degree, then I can hardly imagine she'd be surprised by—"

"Stop. Please. Just no," Ethan laughed. "Her staying here is traumatizing enough. I don't need whatever you're going to say to scar me for life as well."

"Trust me. This isn't my preference, either, to have my boyfriend's mother under the same roof. But the solution was easier than having to check up on her every day, and it allowed her to feel useful watching over you whenever I couldn't," Grady admitted.

"It's just weird. I mean, I get it. But it's weird." Ethan shrugged.

"Too weird to go to bed with me then?" Grady asked, unsuccessfully hiding his disappointment.

"Of course not. I'm not a monk. You have no idea the kinds of things I've been thinking of doing for the past few months." Ethan winked as he stood.

"Oh, I might have a pretty good idea," Grady mused.

"I just hope your room is soundproof because none of them involved sleeping."

Grady was pleased with himself as he also stood to walk them out. "Good. You've already had three months of that. I expect you're well rested and should have all the energy and stamina I require."

Ethan laughed and playfully shoved Grady's back as he followed him out. "You're terrible. I thought you were supposed to be the gentleman."

"I think we both know neither of us is what he appears to be. Isn't that part of the appeal?" Grady smirked, wrapping his arm around Ethan's waist as they headed up the staircase.

"I'll have you know, I'm everything I appear to be," Ethan countered, leaning his head on Grady's shoulder. With that statement, he purposefully produced a pulsing light of blue energy around his body and, just as quickly, retracted the magic back within. "Precisely why you love me. I have nothing to hide."

"Too true. And I want you to show me everything," Grady quipped as they covertly made their way to his room and disappeared inside where they resumed the fiery kiss that had consumed all of their other thoughts.

The aliens and vampires of the multiverse would have to wait. The rest of tonight was reserved for two.

Four: Egos, Dysfunction, and Generally Bad News

"SO, YOU THINK the vampires are organized? Being led by someone?" Ethan asked the following evening. He took a diligent sip of his caramel latte before setting the now empty cup back in the holder of the Jaguar as Grady drove them to his office.

He thoughtfully scrutinized the hand-scrawled pages before him, bound by brass brackets into a manila folder. The files were such an old school way of organizing information and cases, Ethan felt as though he'd been displaced into a seventies detective series. He wondered what Grady might look like with a mustache. Probably as dashing as ever, the dapper devil. He realized he fancied the idea and made a mental note to find a way to persuade him to grow one.

"It's no longer an assumption. I had an admission from one of them last night confirming it," Grady revealed. "I was rather preoccupied afterward, however. Haven't had a chance to update the file." He cast a briefly amused smirk in Ethan's direction.

Ethan snapped the folder shut. "You know, one of these days you should consider joining the modern world and put all of this into a network database. Papers can get lost."

"But they can't get hacked," Grady pointed out as he turned right, down a quiet street. It was early February, and though winter wasn't an actual season in their Texas town, the air was still cool and biting enough that those who didn't have to be out tended to stay indoors.

"You sound like Chris," Grady added. "Which is why such a database is being put together at this very moment without my consent. He'll deny such a thing to my face, but I know him better than to think he'd ever back down when he believes he can eventually persuade me."

He smiled as though reminiscing on some inside joke.

"Who is Chris?" Ethan inquired casually, attempting not to sound too curious.

"My apologies, my head's been in the clouds since you returned. Nothing could be more worth my attention than you," Grady said. "Chris Reed is a new employee. And old...not really friend, mind you, but acquaintance of sorts."

"Ex-boyfriend?" Ethan guessed, his cheeks puffing with mild jealousy.

Grady chuckled. "No. Absolutely not. I don't get involved with everyone I work with, I promise. Nor am I his type. Not by a long shot. Neither is he mine, so you've no reason for such a sour expression."

"Wh—I'm not. Sour... And good. I mean, that he's not...wasn't... Anyway..." Ethan fumbled. He saw Grady suppress an amused grin.

"Yes, anyway..." Grady was kind enough to save him from himself. "With current circumstances such as they are, I needed more help than just Benny, Arthur, and your mother could afford to do. So I called in a favor."

"Right." Ethan winced with self-admonishment. "I guess I didn't realize my taking off would leave you in a lurch. Of course, you'd have to replace me."

"Goodness, no. Don't be daft. You're irreplaceable," Grady corrected. "Vivian was the one who left me in a lurch, as you put it."

"She quit?" Ethan was surprised and then quickly remembered why he shouldn't be so surprised. In truth, he hadn't thought of Vivian Edwards much at all after the incident. Of course, he supposed if he'd been in her shoes, he wouldn't want to try to come back to work and have to face everyone again either. Even if her betrayal happened against her will.

He hated to admit he was relieved. He hadn't known her long enough to trust her, and after what happened, he wasn't sure he ever could. Now, thankfully, the issue was moot.

"To put things simply," Grady confirmed, "I did my best to iron out the awkwardness of the situation, but in the end, she felt too uncomfortable, and I suppose, the line of work was too dangerous. I'm sure her boyfriend, Thomas, had quite a bit of sway in her decision so what was I to do? She loves him, and you can't convince someone to betray the wishes of the person they love. They have to choose that path for themselves."

"So Chris is the new Vivian? Okay." Ethan nodded with acceptance.

"He has a much better rapport with the clients," Grady mused. "And his talents have proved rather invaluable. "

"Right. Because everyone you hire is, in some way, supernatural," Ethan speculated as Grady parked the car in the small lot in front of his office.

"That's not an official qualification. Equal opportunity laws and what not," Grady jested. "But yes, he's a *Magus Machinas.* He prefers the term technomage."

"Is that his motorcycle?" Ethan asked, indicating the sporty-looking silver bike parked beside them.

"Yes," Grady answered. "Hmm...what else should you know? He has blue hair, a few piercings, and several questionable tattoos, but *don't* question him on them. He'll never tell you what they actually mean. Something regarding blood oaths and despotic sorcerer traditions. Rather more old world enigmatic than mystically progressive, if you ask me, but he never does. So, there's that."

"So basically, you've been hanging out with some badass rebellious wizard dude the entire time I was away?" Ethan frowned at him with tentative disapproval and envy.

"A fair assessment, I suppose. Although, it's still up in the air what he's rebelling against," Grady responded evenly.

Ethan tensed with involuntary jealousy.

Grady leaned over to kiss his cheek softly and then whispered in his ear, "You have your aliens; I have my wizards; but most importantly, we have each other. Nothing, nor anyone, ever comes between that. "

"I know." Ethan allowed his demeanor to return to normal.

"Good. Then we shall put any jealous nonsense out of both our, obviously, insecure minds and move forward as though neither of us ever had a silly thought," Grady declared, not unkind but with authority, as he turned off the engine and adjusted his favorite brown cabbie hat.

"Have you ever considered growing a mustache?" Ethan asked as soon as the mention of silly thoughts hit him.

"Bloody hell. Why on earth would I ever want to do *that*?" Grady's nose crinkled in distaste, and he looked Ethan up and down as though he'd gone mad.

"No reason." Ethan dropped the topic and got out of the car; promptly shutting the door before Grady questioned the remark further.

He noticed Grady staring at his reflection in the rearview mirror for a moment and scrunching his upper lip before finally exiting the vehicle. Ethan entered the office with Grady and saw Chris meticulously working at the front desk. The number of computer monitors seemed to have tripled since the last time Ethan had been there, and Chris promptly, and conspicuously, slapped a laptop shut as soon as he saw them arrive.

"Told you he was doing things behind my back," Grady muttered to Ethan with a smug smile as they hung up their jackets.

Everything Grady had said concerning Chris's appearance was correct, Ethan noticed. He stared a bit more than he probably should have. Chris's hair was short, spiky, and a brilliant, bright blue. He had gauged earrings, a nose ring, and a lip ring. He imagined those were just the ones he could see. He also had a tattoo of some indiscernible design on the bottom side of his forearm that flashed into view when his hand rose in greeting. Grady had mentioned more tattoos, but he couldn't see them either and didn't even want to venture to guess how Grady ever had.

Even though Grady and Ethan had removed their outerwear, Chris seemed content to keep his on. He was wearing a black bomber jacket that had vibrant reflective orange stripes on the arms and various patches and logos most probably indicating some organizations Ethan didn't recognize. He also wore black fingerless gloves and a pair of glasses with holographic green coding flashing along them in a long series of scrolling lines. Ethan only saw them for a brief moment before Chris tossed them onto the desktop.

"Holy shit! It's you!" Chris exclaimed, grinning from ear to ear. Ethan realized his reputation preceded him, but he hardly knew what to say in return. That wasn't much of a problem, though, as Chris seemed perfectly fine with a one-sided conversation.

"Dude, I've heard so much about you! It's great to meet you. Awake, anyway," Chris said as he strolled over from behind the desk and bear-hugged Ethan like they were old friends. Thus, ensuring further stunned silence from Ethan.

"Not that I've met you *not* awake." Chris quickly pulled back, holding his gloved hands up as if the gesture would stop any misconstrued assumptions. "I mean, Benny offered, but Grady and I both thought that would be a little weird. I'm not like some creeper or anything. Especially not on some dude I don't know. Not that I would be a creeper on some chick either. I'm not, like, creeper gender-biased."

At this point in his rambling, Chris scratched the back of his neck for a moment, as if forgetting where his train of thought had derailed. He veered back on course with an overly enthusiastic grin. "I've been with your mom!"

"Wh-what?" Ethan managed, horrified.

"I mean, we hang out. A lot. She's shown me some pictures of you. That's how I recognized who you were,"

Chris clarified as he moved on to give Grady a friendly hug and pat on the back in greeting. Ethan wasn't so sure he liked how affectionate Chris was, nor the idea he'd been hugging on his mother, among other disturbing possibilities.

"Yes. Thank you for that—warm welcome, Chris," Grady offered. He stepped back to avoid more imminent hugging as Benny, now in human form, bounded into the room. He'd obviously heard the commotion from his small office in the back.

"Ethan!" he exclaimed, practically bouncing over to hug him as well. Thankfully, this was a hug Ethan felt slightly more comfortable receiving.

"Now I can finally welcome you back without slobbering!" Benny proclaimed happily.

"Always a plus," Ethan mused.

"Benny, did you get Edwin settled in? I left a message for you with Agatha," Grady stated.

"Yeah, yeah." Benny brushed him off, clearly more interested in paying attention to Ethan.

"I've missed having a real friend like you around," Benny continued. "Everyone has been so boring and distracted lately."

"It's called working. You should try it sometime," Grady quipped as he rounded the front desk with Chris, who had signaled for them to follow. Chris gestured to some of the equipment he had set up there. The two quickly immersed themselves in some overtly serious discussion of whatever data Chris had indeed been logging. Grady's expression grew grimmer with each entry Chris referred him to. Graphs, stats, and video recordings hovered off the screens into the air in front of them. They zoomed in and out and minimized upon Chris's simple hand commands. Ethan wondered if this was part of his techno mage abilities or if they were now in command of some highly sophisticated secret government grade technology.

Benny rolled his eyes at them as if the whole display was the dullest thing he'd ever seen. He turned back to Ethan and whispered with a smirk, "See what I mean? *Booor-ing!*"

Ethan chuckled as he and Benny also made their way over to congregate around the conglomeration of devices on the desk. "Only *you* would find magic and vampiric chaos boring," he teased.

"Ugh, vampires. Don't get me started," Benny lamented. "First Dacey. Then that terror horde. And now Mr. Suit-And-Tie von Stuffy McSnob-Face. If I never see another vampire, I will die a happy werehuahua."

"Mac Whozi von Whats-It?" Grady looked up, unsettled.

"I don't know. Some bloodsucker came around asking for you yesterday." Benny flicked his wrist with disinterest.

"And you didn't think to tell me sooner?" Grady demanded.

"I turned into a dog before I had a chance to tell anyone!" Benny defended. "And once I was human again you were...well, busy." He glared back and forth between Grady and Ethan as if they surely understood they were to blame for his lack of communication.

"To be fair, the little yapper here told me this evening as soon as he showed up," Chris intervened. "I was planning to relay the message after we went over these irregularities." He tapped the data report floating above one of the screens. The image warped in toward his fingertip and then back out again as soon as he removed his hand.

"Out with it, then. Who was it?" Grady seemed rabid for pertinent information.

"I can't remember the name exactly. I wrote it down, though." Benny scurried behind the desk to shuffle through a stack of sticky notes haphazardly strewn around. Ethan practically heard Grady's teeth gritting in frustration.

"Like I said. He was wearing an expensive-looking suit and tie and had a snobby attitude to match." Benny described him as he looked for the paper. "His name was von Something-Or-Other. Blond. You know him, I think. He was at the Halloween party."

"Marcus von Rottal," Ethan said, recalling the vampire vividly. Benny appeared to find his note at that exact moment.

"Yes, that was it!" He breathed out in relief as he held the note up. He handed Grady an address with the name. A dark shadow consumed Grady's expression as he read the small yellow paper.

"I remember him," Ethan remarked. "He was Dacey's sire. Left a pretty unforgettable impression, to be honest."

"And now he's made himself at home at Mr. Sinnett's vacant residence," Grady revealed, pocketing the note. Ethan found it odd Grady was referring to his former flame in such a formal manner but kept this thought to himself.

"Did he mention what matter he might have been dropping in on?" Grady pressed.

"No," Benny advised. "He only said he'd be looking for you. Or did he say he'd 'have his eye on you'? Human phrases are weird."

"Dude, you're like the worst secretary ever," Chris criticized with a chuckle as he looked up from one of the monitors.

"I'm not a secretary! I work in the back for a reason. If anyone's a secretary, it's you," Benny defended.

"I am *not* a secretary." Chris took offense and waded up a sticky note, before flicking the crumpled paper at Benny's face.

"Should we go talk to him?" Ethan asked Grady, ignoring the others' antics. If that's how the office had been running since he left, then it was no wonder Grady felt helpless.

"Yes. He must have found out about Dacey. And I'd rather like to question him on current events while we're at it. However, it's still daylight, so we should wait," Grady answered. Ethan noticed he seemed uncharacteristically anxious.

"Great!" Chris intervened, grasping everyone's attention again. "Because I have more bad news that really can't wait."

Five: The Sandman

"WHAT'S THE BAD news?" Grady asked as he turned his attention back to Chris and his conglomeration of computers and devices. The equipment was busily processing various data and seemed to whir and radiate with an alien life of their own.

"Why can't anyone around here ever say, 'Hey, you know what? I have great news!'" Ethan jokingly mumbled. He leaned over the counter, lifting up on his toes a bit, and rested on his elbows to get a better look at Chris's setup. He wouldn't admit it to the mage's face—he wasn't entirely sure whether or not he liked him yet—but he was extremely interested in his technological witchcraft.

Benny sighed audibly to let everyone know his disdain for work babble and retreated back to his office. If he wasn't interested in work, Ethan speculated at what he actually spent his time doing back there. *I bet he spends the day watching YouTube videos of cats.*

"We're not going to be able to launch an attack at the vampire's source," Chris began to explain. He waved his hand in front of one of the monitors and a holographic map of the town displayed in front of him. The map slowly rotated counterclockwise, and Ethan noticed various quadrants had red orbs, like pinpoints, affixed to them. Each region of town also pulsed with a vast variant spectrum of colors.

"Why not?" Grady said, inspecting the map closely. Unlike Ethan, he appeared to understand what he was looking at.

"There isn't one," Chris divulged in a matter-of-fact tone. "At least not in Shady Pines. We're not dealing with locals. As you know, I've set surveillance along any ley lines and key paranormal hot spots. Nothing. Well, nothing vampiric, at any rate. Which leads me to believe they're entering town after nightfall and leaving before dawn. "

"I suspected as much," Grady sighed. "Without being able to trail them or capture one and implement a proper interrogation, we'll never find out who is organizing them or what they're after."

"Maybe Mr. von Vampire will have an answer for us," Chris suggested in reference to Benny's visitor.

"You think they're after something?" Ethan asked.

"Or someone," Grady mumbled.

"What's happening with the psychokinetic energy levels?" Grady gestured to the pulsing multicolored stats. "Why are they so erratic? "

"That's the other thing I wanted to show you," Chris said as he waved his wrist again. The revolution of the map sped up, and he held both hands together, touching his index fingers to the opposing thumbs, and then pulled them apart slowly. This caused the map to zoom in to the portion of town where they were currently located.

"Notice how their regulation is even around the rest of town?" he continued. "But then they blowout in these irregular variances within a ten-mile radius of a focused center? I believe they're reacting to a mobile catalyst. It's disrupting the natural state of the energy surrounding it. Causing the area's usually stable psychokinetic levels to become...well...unstable. "

"Have you isolated the catalyst? Do we know what it is?" Grady pressed.

"It's him," Chris stated tentatively, as he gestured across the countertop to Ethan. He minimized the map and returned the data to its monitor of origin.

"Me?" Ethan was rendered with immediate bewilderment. "So, is that...bad?"

"Is there any way to discern if this has always been the effect of his presence?" Grady seemed overcome by the possibilities. "Or is it due to his recent interdimensional travels? Could this be why Shady Pines has drawn in so many supernaturals? You're practically a beacon. Suppose that's how the vampires found you. But then, that wouldn't make sense either, unless you were affecting the levels while you slept as well. Though, you'd think the vampires would've shown up at my doorstep. Everyone else seems to be doing so."

Ethan sensed Grady's mounting frustration as more questions than answers started piling up.

"Wait, you think the vampires are here for *me*?" Ethan was used to yielding to onslaughts of wildly unbelievable information regarding himself; the surreal had been a constant in his life for the past several months and part of the territory when it came to spending time with Grady. But even he needed a breather between revelations every now and then.

"Just a theory," Grady admitted.

"Honestly, there's no way to know if Ethan has always had this effect on the environment or if it's a new development. No one was monitoring him before," Chris answered the first questions. "I think it's a fair assumption that altering reality around him must be normal for his species."

"My *species*," Ethan repeated with sudden irritation. He couldn't quite put his finger on why but Chris's implication that he wasn't human annoyed him.

"Somnium Viators," Chris replied pragmatically, not appearing to catch the crossness in Ethan's tone. "Descendants of the Sandman."

"He knows what he is," Grady intervened. "I think the implications of what we've learned here need some time to process. For all of us." The conversation was interrupted by an entrance through the office's front door. Karen Roam carried in two coffees from the nearby cafe, which Ethan immediately found suspicious.

"MILF alert," Chris mumbled to the other men in a singsong voice.

Ethan turned to him with an expression that endeavored to kill. And with the vast list of new supernatural powers he'd been discovering lately, he wouldn't be surprised if that might realistically be possible.

"Sorry, man." Chris quickly tried to save face. "You're, um… You're not usually here."

"Stay away from my mom," Ethan warned in a steely tone, out of Karen's earshot.

Grady appeared to stifle a laugh and turned to greet their new arrival.

"Karen! Good evening. You look lovely, as usual." Grady brandished a charming smile and gave her small, but curvy, feminine frame a friendly hug as she approached.

"Thank you, Grady." Karen beamed, returning the hug. She did look lovely and relaxed in a simple green-and-black plaid button-up, jeans, and brown riding boots.

Her big blue eyes immediately settled on her son and she practically radiated joy as she attempted to embrace him, too, with both coffees still in hand. "I can't tell you how happy it makes me to have you back, sweetheart," she gushed.

"It's a little surreal to see you *here*," Ethan admitted warmly. It was the first time they were both together in Grady's offbeat office.

"It is for me too," she admitted. And then to Ethan's horror, she handed off her extra coffee to Chris who responded with "Thanks, love. "

"When I wasn't watching over you at Grady's, I spent most of my time here doing research and learning everything from Chris. He's quite brilliant," she explained and then smiled, a bit too cheerfully for Ethan's liking, at the blue-haired mage.

"Great" was the only response Ethan was able to muster at the idea, and his tone was fretfully unenthusiastic.

"It *is* great. Now that she doesn't have to watch over you, she can spend more time here with me," Chris added, winking at Karen. He took a sip of the coffee and went back to analyzing his data without a blink in Ethan's direction.

Ethan wasn't sure if Chris was joking simply to irritate him, or if everyone was so comfortable with this dynamic already casual flirtation was simply second nature to them. Either way, Ethan decided, right then and there, he didn't like Chris. He couldn't imagine what his mom was thinking. She hadn't moved on the entire time after his father had died, so why now? Why *this* guy?

His vexing thoughts must have been easy to read on his face as, once again, Grady intervened as the diplomat.

"Your mother is a quick study," he complimented, taking care to position himself closer to Ethan to express his solidarity. "I think she'd be perfectly capable of managing this place for us if she'd ever take up my offer."

"I'm still considering the idea," she replied sweetly as she took a seat next to Chris. Her ease of comfort around the mage was making Ethan increasingly uncomfortable. He scrutinized Chris's appearance again, trying to see past the blue hair, piercings, and tattoos he never would have imagined his mother could be attracted to.

Chris was tall, fairly fit, and in his own way, handsome, Ethan supposed. Probably in his early to mid-thirties if he had to venture a guess. Plus, he was capable of some pretty impressive magic. He could understand the appeal, but he didn't have to like it. Especially not from his mom. She wasn't supposed to find anyone but his father appealing. And she certainly wasn't allowed to fawn over anyone.

He realized how ridiculous that sounded, and he pushed his thoughts aside before he started to chide himself for being selfish. He didn't want to like Chris, so he wouldn't, and that was that.

"Sunset," Grady noted, glancing out the window. "We'll be able to head out soon. Perhaps we'll finally have a semi-reasonable suspect to interrogate, after all."

"Where are you going?" Karen inquired, glancing to Ethan with motherly concern.

"A vampire appears to want our attention," Grady answered. "Hopefully, unlike the rest we've dealt with recently, he'll be civil."

"He seemed all right. At the party," Ethan added. "I mean; he came across as a total snob, but he was nice to me before he left. Paid me a lot of compliments."

Grady frowned, but if he had any personal opinions on the matter, he certainly didn't voice them.

"So, you know him?" Karen prodded. She looked to Grady with worry. "Is it necessary for Ethan to go with you? He just got back. Maybe he should take it easy."

"He's perfectly capable of protecting himself. And me too, for that matter," Grady stated with pride.

Ethan had shown him a few tricks the night before, so Grady had a much better idea of his powers now and how to utilize them. While the context, at the time, was entirely different, he imagined Grady still theorized the possible practical applications. However, none would be quite as satisfying for either of them as the ways in which he implemented them in bed. But no one else needed to be privy to those details.

"Show her," Grady urged Ethan with a knowing smile.

Ethan held out his hands and concentrated inwardly on his own energy until the magic felt like a centered adaptable mass inside his body. He willed the power to move through his limbs and push outward from within himself, causing a vibrant flux of what appeared as blue light to emerge from his palms. They tingled as he let the energy morph and grow into a pulsing shield of milky cyan energy around him. The haziness of the mass began to sharpen until it took on the visible qualities of stardust.

"Go ahead, touch him," Grady instructed Karen, who was wide-eyed with fascination.

She slowly rose to her feet and brushed her long auburn hair back behind her ears as she approached her son. She was seeing him now for the first time as the creature he truly was. More than just a cosmic bubble encased him now. His entire body was translucent. He had transformed into a sandman.

Karen took a shaky emotional breath and carefully reached out to touch her son. Part of Ethan's energy attached itself with hers, taking away all pain, discomfort, and sadness within her. He willed her into a blissful state of dreaming.

When he let go of her hand, the energy and its effects returned to Ethan; demonstrating they were only available through contact.

Karen covered her mouth with shock. "My God…" was all she said. Her eyes welled up with tears.

"Now you." Grady nodded at Chris to do the same. Ethan noticed a mischievous smile adorned Grady's lips which gave him a pretty good inkling of the kind of experience he should demonstrate for Chris.

Chris strolled over with ignorant confidence. He reached forward to take Ethan's hand, and as soon as he came in contact with him, Ethan shot dark dream energy through him that knocked Chris back several feet, causing him to topple over the waiting room chairs.

"Chris!" Karen ran to his side to help him up and check that he was okay.

"I'm all right. Just a little jolt of negative dream energy. Should have expected that," Chris reassured her, as he stood from the toppled office furniture. He rubbed his right elbow, which had taken most of the impact of the collision.

Ethan returned to his human form, and Grady joined him in a fit of immature laughter.

"Ethan Roam!" Karen attempted to scold him but, poorly suppressing a smile, ultimately found the humor in the situation too.

"Yes, yes. Very hilarious. You're my worst nightmare. I get it." Chris rolled his eyes and marched back to his computers. This time, he slumped into his chair looking sufficiently knocked down a few pegs.

"Like I said, Ethan can handle himself," Grady insisted. "Now, we'd better get going. Though civil, I have a feeling Marcus might not be as loose with information as Dacey once was."

"Well, you could always blast it out of him," Chris muttered under his breath, returning his attention to his computers.

"Go ahead. We've got everything under control here," Karen assured them.

Obviously wanting to avoid eye contact, Chris focused on his work. Ethan imagined the only thing more bruised than his elbow was his ego. He let himself enjoy his petty triumph for now.

Six: A High Stakes Gamble

AS THEY MERGED into the slow flow of traffic onto Main Street, Grady eventually broke the awkward silence that had filled the space between them since they'd gotten in the car.

"Don't be too hard on Chris," Grady advised, still smiling. "He really is a good guy."

"So says you," Ethan responded. He realized he'd been slouching while pouting, so he sat a little straighter and wiped his sweaty palms across the knees of his jeans. He always became nervous whenever Grady seemed to know what he was thinking.

"And is my word not good enough?" Grady raised an eyebrow.

Ethan simply shrugged in reluctant deferment and stared out the passenger window at the shops as they passed by. Most had already closed before nightfall. Only the restaurants and bars braved the dangers of the night in Shady Pines. The general public wasn't aware of the supernatural population—at least not officially—but there were a lot of rumors and enough unsolved crimes to make most people wary. However, there were always those souls, adept at revelry, willing to risk any danger for good food, drinks, and the prospect of a wild night out. Those few tended to travel in groups and were the only ones walking the sidewalks between venues at the current hour.

Until this very moment, it hadn't occurred to Ethan he would never be one of them. Fully human, of legal drinking age, single, and blissfully unaware of the truth of the universe surrounding them; he'd never just be a college guy out with friends, carousing, and exploring the dating scene. It was a future most people grow up expecting as an inevitability of youthful adulthood, but his life had been hijacked before he'd even had his first beer. Now...well, now, he'd already traveled to realms they would never even know existed.

He'd never felt so disconnected from his home as he did right then. His hometown. His home planet. His home species. He was an outsider, a god among men. And yet if any of them looked his way, they would never know. He'd only seem like the awkward wallflower he'd always been.

He hadn't considered his perspective would change so drastically when he returned. Nor that things would be so different. He felt foolish now, thinking everything would have stayed the same. His cheeks flushed with embarrassment at his own naivety and selfish annoyance that his loved ones hadn't had the decency to spare any drastic life decisions until he got back.

"Is my mom really dating him?" Ethan asked, still staring out the window but clenching his fists slightly, for lack of a better way to control his emotions. He didn't need his supernatural energy bubbling up and causing the interior of their car to glow like he was hosting his own personal rave party in the passenger seat.

"Not officially," Grady consoled. "In truth, I'm not sure anything romantic has transpired between them. Although, I wouldn't swear to it. They've worked alone together on more than one occasion and I'm not Chris's keeper. Nor your mother's for that matter."

He glanced toward Ethan at the latter statement as if to quietly insinuate neither was Ethan.

"I think it's quite apparent they're drawn to each other," he continued. "For what it's worth, he seems to make her happy. "

Ethan relaxed slightly as his boyfriend talked. His soothing voice and reasonable wisdom always found a way to anchor him. It was one of the many things he cherished about Grady. In that way, at least, he didn't feel like an outsider. The love and admiration he felt for Grady helped him remain connected to the world and to his own humanity.

"I guess..." Ethan reluctantly agreed. He attempted to be open-minded but let out a heavy sigh. "I guess it was stupid to think she'd never move on to someone else. It's just...well, she *hadn't*."

"If I may impart an observation based on personal experience?" Grady offered. Curious as to what he had to say on the subject, Ethan looked to him expectantly.

"It's not so much 'moving on' as continuing to live. Love is not something that's replicated. It is entirely unique any time one experiences it. And one love does not degrade or negate the value of another. As you know, life can take some dark turns. But our endless capacity for love ultimately keeps us on course; so long as we're willing to let it." Grady proffered a gentle smile.

Ethan nodded, accepting Grady's wisdom. He understood the subtle parallel Grady had drawn between his and Karen's experiences. How could Ethan possibly argue with such raw sincerity?

In an attempt to lighten the mood, Ethan teased, "If the whole paranormal psychiatrist, alternative healer, slash hunter thing doesn't work out for you, then I have great faith you could land a solid career in the greeting card or self-help calendar industries."

Grady chuckled as they pulled up the drive to a Victorian-style cottage in the oldest part of town. Ethan turned his attention to the house. He was fascinated to see the place where Dacey, his former eccentric vampire friend, once called home. It was more humble in appearance than he'd expected, given Dacey's flashy nature and typical opulent tastes. The original windows, of which there were only two, were intact but boarded up from the inside; which was understandable and common with vampires. The paint of the house had probably once been a pleasant blue but had faded to gray. It was well-kept, overall, but the general mood was a house that appeared as much in mourning of its former tenant as everyone else was.

A small pebble pathway led from the drive to the porch and, although there were no other vehicles in sight, the front porch light was on as if they were expected; perhaps they were. Otherwise, the property held no visible signs anyone else was there.

Ethan turned to see Grady staring hesitantly at the front door. He wondered if he was trying to make up his mind about this particular house call. Then he wondered how many times Grady had been here before—had walked through that door before—under circumstances he'd rather not dwell on.

An uneasy pang of jealousy hit the pit of his stomach, and he tried to push the feeling down. Suddenly the talk of *endless capacity to love* felt less reassuring.

"What do you think Marcus wants?" Ethan asked to break the mounting tension.

"Well…" Grady sighed, still staring at the house. "He's Dacey's sire, so I doubt he's here to actually help us. I'd have to venture to guess he either wants to kill us in retaliation for Dacey's death or he's attempting a power play for a new progeny. One who would be a more than suitable replacement."

Grady then looked at Ethan pointedly as he turned the key to shut off the car's engine.

"*What? Me?*" Ethan was floored. "You think he wants to make me a vampire?"

"I think he wants recompense. He has refined tastes. And you're quite valuable," Grady answered. His distrust of Marcus was readily apparent. "So play your cards close to your vest and remember Marcus is *not* Dacey, if you catch my meaning."

Perplexed, Ethan watched as Grady exited the car and straightened his cabbie hat with a determined look. Ethan stumbled out of the car and over his words with an equal lack of grace. "Cards? Grady, what are you talking about?"

Grady approached the house, offering no further information.

They didn't have to wait long to be greeted by Dacey's sire. Marcus von Rottal was quick to answer the door, but despite his having summoned their presence, he seemed a bit distracted.

"You came," he stated with only mild surprise, as if he'd expected they'd fear him too much to actually show up. Then, with a flippantly disinterested gesture, he indicated for them to come inside. When they did, Ethan politely shut the door behind them. Marcus was already striding down the short main hall into a bedroom.

"This way," he commanded them, expecting the two to follow his lead. Although he appeared as handsome and youthful as the last time they'd seen him, his face was worn with dismay. His amber eyes were dulled and his honey-golden locks were a curled, disheveled mess atop his head.

His fitted, cornflower-blue button-up shirt hadn't been entirely fastened all the way, and the long sleeves hung loosely around his pale arms. White suspenders, not having been strapped up, hung from his gray slacks. He wore no shoes but did have on a matching pair of blue pinstripe socks. It was as though he'd been in the middle of dressing, or undressing, and had then forgotten the process entirely while becoming preoccupied with matters of greater importance. Which, for a vampire, must have been significant as there were few things more important to them than their appearance.

The preoccupation had apparently taken form in the manner of scouring all of Dacey's belongings. Drawers to his dresser hung open with their contents mussed. Wooden crates, trunks, and cardboard boxes lined the floor and were piled on the bed. Most were open and had already been inspected and others sat, still fastened shut, awaiting their turn to be explored. Letters were also scattered, and a journal had been open and flipped, spine-side up, to mark the reader's current place. They had obviously interrupted this process of sentimental excavation as Marcus went right back to work sifting through the contents of a small, black-leather trunk atop Dacey's bed.

"I must admit, I'm surprised you came willingly," Marcus confessed as he slid open the silken ties of a crimson satin pouch and looked inside. Apparently, its contents didn't divulge what he was hoping they would, and he promptly retied the small bag and dropped it back in the trunk. "I thought I'd have to make another formal visit. Perhaps even schedule an appointment. You keep yourself very busy, *doctor*," he added, some harshness implied in the delivery of the latter statement. However, he remained engulfed in his investigation and afforded neither of them so much as a glance.

"Indeed I do. I'm sure you're aware of precisely how *busy* things have been lately" was Grady's guarded reply. "However, I felt we owed you the courtesy."

Ethan edged a step out from behind Grady, standing beside him now. He observed the state of the room. The bedroom was fairly decent in size, and the decor was definitely suited to Dacey's tastes. He'd always had a flair for the dramatic and enjoyed playing up his own vampire vibe no matter how cliché. Accordingly, everything was crimson and black and heavily influenced by the Victorian era. The room was an idealized setting for a gothic romantic tryst, which made Ethan a little uncomfortable knowing he was the only man currently present who had not partaken in one on the premises. Although, it hadn't been for lack of invitation.

It was Ethan's forward motion into the room that prompted Marcus to give up searching through Dacey's belongings and turn to them with his full attention. His eyes were inquisitively trained on Ethan while he responded to Grady.

"I have no idea what you mean on either count," he said evenly, placing his hands on his hips as though they were now wasting his time. Despite the mannerism, his interest remained focused on Ethan.

The fixation was mutual. He knew his own power could protect him should anything go awry, yet he still perceived Marcus as an intimidating figure. Perhaps because Grady was so distrusting of him or because of his own guilt concerning Dacey's death. Or maybe his intimidation was because of the way Marcus's fitted shirt stretched and tugged when he moved his arms, causing the few buttons which were fastened to strain against his slim and muscled torso rendering Ethan unable to not have improper thoughts at such an improper time.

The vampiric Adonis was practically ripping through his soul with his ardent gaze, and Ethan was powerless to the reverberating echoes of his own heart beginning to slam against his chest. He worried Marcus sensed his nervousness too.

"I think you do, but if you'd rather play coy, then that's entirely understandable, given the circumstances," Grady countered. "Although, your ignorance leads me to question why you'd want to meet with us at all."

Now Grady had the vampire's attention. Marcus's gaze broke from assessing Ethan and turned on him with ferocity.

"This visit is no mere courtesy!" he snapped. Ethan now noticed the dark circles beneath his ageless amber eyes. They were sunken in as a human's would be had they been crying for hours or attempting to function on a severe lack of sleep. He wondered what similar instance might negatively affect a vampire's health or appearance. At any rate, Marcus looked the part of the tormented man.

"I am owed an explanation!" Marcus continued. His voice was strained with rage and sadness. "You lost him! He trusted you and you *used* him! "

"I did nothing of the sort," Grady countered boldly. "Your progeny knew the risks of our arrangement and made his own decisions."

"Dacey!" Marcus threw one of the open-and-already-ransacked boxes in Grady's direction. Grady dodged the object expertly, and the contents inside smashed on impact as they hit the floor.

"His name is *Dacey*, you arrogant prick!" Marcus wailed.

And then something truly disturbing happened. Ethan witnessed a vampire cry. Or the closest thing one might come to crying. Marcus's eyes reddened with tears of blood, and he tried to wipe them away with the backs of his hands, smearing stains on his porcelain skin and soaking the cuffs of his sleeves in crimson. His grief was a horrific sight. He began pacing in the limited space and then turned on Grady with murderous rage.

"He's gone because of *you*!" His voice cracked and choked with anguished sorrow. "You *fucked* him, and you won't even say his name?"

For a split second, Ethan thought he'd have to save Grady from an attack, but instead of charging at him, Marcus stumbled backward and let an open spot on the bed catch his mourning body. He slumped dejectedly, trying to fight back his sobbing. Sounding entirely offended, Marcus muttered, "He won't even say his name..."

Who knew a vampire's heart could break? Shameful, Ethan glanced at Grady. Grady didn't seem shocked, or even remotely sympathetic; at best, he only seemed suspicious. Ethan guessed Grady might assume this was an act. Grady's prerogative was to expect the worst from supernaturals. But Ethan wasn't so jaded. Marcus's pain seemed pure and real, and Ethan imagined how devastated he, too, would be if he had lost Grady in the same way. He hoped he'd never have to experience such tragedy.

Ethan walked forward, cautiously approaching Marcus, who was still sobbing and trying madly to wipe away his ruby tears.

"Ethan..." Grady's hushed tone warned he was stumbling too close to a viper.

Gathering courage, Ethan knelt before Marcus and rested comforting hands on the vampire's knees. Intimidating or not, Marcus had lost someone he loved and Ethan believed they owed him, at the very least, their sympathy.

"Dacey was the bravest man I've ever known," Ethan said. "It's not Grady's fault he's gone. It's mine. He destroyed himself to save me, and I promise you I will never forget that. If it weren't for his selflessness, I would be dead."

Marcus had immediately fallen silent the moment Ethan touched him. He kept further tears restrained with a heavy breath. His bloodshot eyes were now locked with Ethan's, most likely assessing him for sincerity. He seemed satisfied Ethan's compassion was real.

Marcus lifted his hand to gently trace the outline of Ethan's brow, running his fingertips along his cheekbone as though memorizing him through his touch.

His hands were still covered in blood, and Ethan felt the substance being lightly smeared on his face. He might have been disgusted under different circumstances, but instead, he was oddly at ease. There was a commonality between his guilt and Marcus's pain. They knew nothing of one another, were in no way alike, but he felt linked to him through mutual loss.

"I'm really sorry," Ethan continued, sensing he had made some progress with Marcus. "Believe me. If we could have stopped things from happening the way they did, we would have. If Grady could have saved him, he would have. If I could bring him back, I would."

"You would," Marcus repeated, a quiet hollow echo of hope. His bloody tears had stopped.

"We all lost him that day. He meant something special to each of us," Ethan insisted.

"Some more so than others." Marcus patted Ethan's hand limply and took the opportunity to glare at Grady with contempt.

Grady stood unwavering but gritted his teeth. He wished with all his heart Ethan would stop being such a sympathetic fool. While his empathy was part of what made him the incredible soul he was, he didn't want anyone to take advantage of that. Least of all a deranged vampire with Mr. Darcy-esque appeal. The entire situation was as volatile as he'd feared, and Grady began to doubt the potential payoff of his risk in allowing this meeting to happen. Marcus still hadn't confessed anything worthwhile.

"Is that why you led the other vampires to Shady Pines?" Grady pressed, eager to break whatever deviant notions Marcus might be having regarding Ethan. "To seek revenge? To destroy us? "

"What are you talking about, you insipid fool?" Marcus narrowed his eyes and pulled back from Ethan. Ethan took the cue to step aside.

"Oh, please." Grady rolled his eyes at Marcus in annoyance as he fished his handkerchief out of his pocket and handed it over to Ethan to clean his face. "Spare us the act of innocence. You're incapable of selling it. We both know you have to be aware of the other vampires in town. They're a complete nuisance and have been wreaking havoc for months. "

"As a matter of fact, I *wasn't* aware," Marcus said, his composure now regained. He remained sitting. "I've only ventured outdoors once—to contact you. Excuse me, if I've been too busy grieving to waste my precious time concerning myself with the current events of your dull little town. "

"Is that why you look like you're next in line for Death? You haven't been feeding?" Grady assessed. "How long has it been?"

Marcus glared at him as though he were rude for prying and gave no answer.

"How did you find out about Dacey?" Ethan asked.

"Only a handful of people knew what happened that night. And in the end, Grady and I were the only ones there."

"I don't know everything," Marcus admitted. His demeanor shifted. He appeared more open and approachable. Clearly, he preferred dealing with Ethan at this point. He'd most likely prefer to have Grady leave if the choice were up to him.

"In an effort to extend an olive branch of information and establish a gentlemen's agreement of honesty between us, I'll admit to having had a spy in your midst for quite some time," Marcus revealed.

"What?" Grady was caught off guard by this revelation, which seemed to please Marcus. The vampire produced a self-satisfied smirk.

"Do you honestly think I'd let someone as priceless as Dacey leave my radar for one second?" Marcus replied. "Of course not. Obviously, you're aware of how valuable he is. You kept him *intimately* close. I've had eyes watching him for me since the moment he took permanent residence here. How was I to know then that her eventually collaborating with you would lead to his demise?"

"Vivian." Grady realized. As he thought back over the past several years, the pieces started to fall into place, and he felt like the foolish man Marcus accused him of being. He explained to Ethan, "She was the one who first informed me about Dacey. Explicitly insisted on my meeting him. We enlisted his help with our work together. It never occurred to me she only wanted to keep him under her own watchful eye."

"An unfortunate turn of events for all of us: her deciding to involve you. If I were to take revenge on anyone, she would be among the first. But contrary to what you think of me, I'm not a savage," Marcus added with distaste. "Enlisting the services of that little witch is one of the worst decisions I've ever made. The worst, of course, was letting Dacey go in the first place. I only did so because I thought he'd eventually come back."

"But Vivian wasn't there when Dacey died. Thomas took her to safety before he went through the portal," Ethan interjected before Marcus was able to get off track again.

"Which is what brings the circle round," Marcus sighed. "Vivian confessed but lacked details. I had to contact one or both of you. Obviously, I would have preferred *not* to deal with the doctor." He sneered at Grady and then looked back to Ethan. "But you were missing in action. Glad to know you're all right. Grady has a tendency to lose those more valuable than himself."

"Mind your tongue," Grady warned.

"Or what? You'll kill me too? Add another corpse to your tally?" Marcus shot back.

"Stop!" Ethan stood between them. "We'll never get anywhere like this. You two were both loved by the same man and now he's gone. I get it. That sucks and I'm sorry. But you can't hold Dacey against each other forever, or we'll never get anywhere. We all want something out of this situation, so can we please just work out a solution? Preferably one without any dead bodies?"

"But you didn't love him. Did you?" Marcus challenged Grady. His tone indicated he already knew the answer. "You were toying with him. Stringing him along for your own personal gain. Making him think you cared while you fine-tuned him into another disposable supernatural weapon for your arsenal. He told me all about you. You and your war against the monsters of the world. Tell me, how is that going? My guess is not well."

Grady stayed silent, despite his mounting rage, so as not to play into his trap.

"You said you were offering an olive branch of honesty," Ethan prompted. "Well, we accept. We came to give you our condolences and to, hopefully, find out any information to do with the vampire outbreak, which you've since confessed you know nothing of. So, tell us, what were *you* hoping to get out of this meeting?"

Marcus appeared to silently evaluate Ethan again and seemed exceedingly pleased with whatever he'd discerned from him. He looked to Grady with haughty opinion. "Ah. I see you've found a more powerful weapon. Bear in mind, you don't deserve this one either."

"On that, we can agree. Though, he's not a weapon. He's a blessing. And I'm extremely thankful he sees better in me than the rest of the world." Grady smiled tensely at Ethan for reassurance.

"Hmm...Dacey seemed to think you worthy of his adoration as well, for whatever daft reason," Marcus said, rolling his eyes a bit with a disapproving shake of his head but his demeanor calmed. Now completely composed, Marcus answered Ethan's question.

"What I wanted was to know exactly how it happened," he said. "Did Dacey have anything with him? Something you may have mistaken for a weapon? Did he give any specific instructions?"

"No. He didn't have a weapon. Unless you count his fangs. What kind of instructions?" Ethan attempted to recall. He then retold the werewolf attack in lengthy detail. How Dacey fought Marius, the werewolf who had escaped from the Dream World to enslave Ethan. That he encouraged Ethan to open a portal and then led Marius into another dimension. And how the wolf had grabbed onto Dacey at the last second and taken him along. Ethan was unable to hold back his own guilt-ridden tears as he recounted how difficult closing up the portal had been, knowing he'd sealed someone else's fate in an effort to save his own life. He revealed making that decision was the single worst moment of his own existence.

Unexpectedly, Marcus strode forward and gave Ethan a hug. Grady monitored the embrace with extreme scrutiny, ready to intervene, in case it turned into a surprise attack. It didn't.

Marcus pulled back and wiped the wet confessions from Ethan's cheeks. Which only stained them with blood again.

"Thank you! You've said precisely what I needed to hear," he expressed as his anxiety apparently began to lift. His amber eyes were no longer dull. They twinkled with renewed optimism.

"I don't understand," Ethan said, his voice shaky. Grady was confused as well. Marcus was more unpredictable than he'd calculated, and it was making him all the more uneasy.

"Of course, you don't, you brilliant thing." Marcus beamed and gave Ethan's shoulders a pat. In fact, he seemed downright giddy. "Of course, you don't!" Now, he was laughing, hopefully with relief, like a madman.

"I think Marcus needs some time alone," Grady advised Ethan under his breath in caution. *Best not to stay in the presence of a supernatural lunatic for any prolonged period of time.*

Marcus was crying again, but this time they appeared to be tears of happiness. Although, why he was happy was anyone's guess, but the crying did remind him to wipe his own face off again.

"Thank you for your time, Mr. von Rottal." Grady attempted to end the visit cordially. "If you do find yourself possessing any information on our vampire outbreak, please, do impart the information our way."

"Yes! Yes, of course." Marcus nodded vigorously. He made a point to hug Ethan once more on their way out and whispered, not nearly quiet enough, "Thank you again, Ethan Roam. You've improved my prospects tenfold. I'll see you again soon. Very soon."

"Uh, good. I mean, you're welcome." Ethan wore a nervous smile as they stepped out onto the porch. Marcus didn't give Grady any sort of farewell and generally acted like he was no longer there. He smirked seductively at Ethan, bid him a good night, and then slammed the door in their faces.

Ethan wondered aloud, "What do you think he was looking for in those boxes?"

Grady took Ethan by the hand and quickly led him down the drive to the car.

"Of all things, *that's* what you're concerned about? Bloody vampires!" He cursed under his breath as he stormed beside the vehicle. Pointing a finger at Ethan, he demanded, "Do me a favor and stay away from him."

"Me?" Ethan produced an awkward laugh.

A red flag went up for Grady as Ethan no longer seemed to see the vampire as a threat.

"I'm pretty sure it was you he didn't like," Ethan teased as they got in the car.

"Precisely. And he likes you *too* much," Grady stated, tossing his cabbie hat onto the dash in frustration before hurriedly whipping the car away from the premises. Bringing that bloodthirsty monster and his dream traveler together had been a foolhardy risk. He'd been stupid to assume Ethan wouldn't be so blatantly manipulated. As much as he hated to acknowledge the fact, manipulation of Ethan's trusting nature was precisely how their own lives had ended up entwined. He couldn't drive away from this bad decision fast enough.

Ethan remained silent as they drove, allowing Grady time to regain his composure.

Grady hoped Ethan would heed his warning but sensed his inherent empathy for others might be too hard to dissuade. He knew from experience Ethan had a soft heart for broken men. He also knew the look in a vampire's eyes when they were on the hunt for something.

Ultimately, Ethan would always remain the unknown variable. But Grady was certain of one thing in this equation. Marcus was a predator who had effectively evaluated his prey.

Seven: The Hunter & His Weapon

"HAVE I DISAPPOINTED you in some way?" Ethan spoke up after a few minutes of intense silence. Grady was brooding and driving, which wasn't the safest combination.

"Don't be absurd." Grady brushed the accusation off. "The problem isn't you. There's quite a bit at stake at the moment, and I'm struggling to discern facts from paranoia."

"You do seem uptight. More so than usual," Ethan assessed. He glanced at Grady with mild concern, wishing psychic powers were part of his quickly stockpiling supernatural repertoire. Unfortunately, wishing things into reality wasn't either. He was a sandman; not a genie.

"Perhaps because I have more to lose than I ever have before." Grady bestowed a small, encouraging smile in his direction.

"At this point, *your* safety is more of a concern than mine," Ethan insisted. "I know in your mind I'm still that awkward defenseless guy you took under your wing, but a lot has changed. I've changed. I'm, well... I'm still awkward." He gave a short self-deprecating laugh before continuing. "But I can take care of myself. I don't want you to view me as your responsibility. I want you to see me as your equal."

"But we're not equal, Ethan," Grady insisted, keeping his eyes fixed steadily on the dimly lit road. "That's rather the point."

"Because you still think I'm inexperienced." Ethan pouted. He was annoyed by the thought.

"No. Because you're valuable. And I'm expendable. No, I am," Grady countered, cutting off Ethan's start of a protest. "You *are* my responsibility, whether you like that fact or not. I know you're powerful. I know you can hold your own in a fight. But you can't take on the world alone, Ethan, and believe me, you'll feel like you're doing exactly that one day. And I'll be your first line of defense. You must let me protect you because I'm going to do so with or without your permission."

"Damn. Chivalry may be out of style, but it certainly isn't dead." Ethan grinned.

"Not while I still breathe, it's not." Grady smiled with affection, his weary but soulful eyes wrinkled sweetly at the edges.

"You two are so adorable! My forever OTP," an energized voice broke through their shared moment. Ethan looked down to discover the intrusion was coming from a magic-imbued holographic screen on the dashboard, which he hadn't noticed before. Probably because the screen *was* magic and hadn't been there until the techno-mage willed it to be. His face was smiling brightly back at them as he wiggled his gloved fingers in a smarmy wave at Ethan.

"Chris. We really must work on your concept of privacy and the fact that you seem to have none." Grady rolled his eyes with bemusement.

"Yeah, well, when you have the ability to hack into literally anything in the world, you come to realize privacy is a pipe dream of the masses," Chris responded. "Also, we have a problem."

"I'm certain I'd hear from you a lot less if you'd only contact me when we *don't* have a problem." Grady pointed out.

"So, I take it you guys handled that Marcus guy just fine. You're both still alive and appear to have all of your appendages intact," Chris mused as he elbowed a curious Benny, who was peeking over his shoulder, out of the way. "Which is great because you have a few more vamps to visit tonight."

"Hmm. Looks like I'll get to see your powers in action after all," Grady said to Ethan. Then back to Chris, he requested, "Map coordinates. We're on our way."

"You got it," Chris replied and a second semitransparent screen popped up beside him depicting a street map of the town. A swirling vortex of blue stars acted as a beacon and pinpointed their destination.

"Hey, do you mind if I order pizzas with your card?" Chris asked, already pulling up a menu on a nearby computer.

"You ask like I could stop you," Grady said.

"Hey, I may not be a lot of things, but I am polite. Occasionally," Chris defended.

"Chicken spinach alfredo for me," Grady quickly threw out his order and looked to Ethan.

"Pepperoni," Ethan answered.

"And a pepperoni," Grady repeated as if Chris didn't hear Ethan say so himself. Chris gave them a thumbs-up and then shut off his feed, leaving only the screen with the map. Grady mumbled jokingly, "Really? Pepperoni? For a man of infinite options, you certainly keep your choices basic."

"Did you just call me basic?" Ethan scoffed.

Grady hit the brakes, and the tires squealed across

the pavement as he skidded to a stop beside an antique furniture store, which had already closed for the night. He promptly turned off the engine. The magical screen indicating they were at their destination blipped away as if it never existed. Grady nodded toward the building, which had a noticeably broken window.

"They're not always the brightest creatures, are they?" Grady asked rhetorically. "A furniture store. Full of wooden objects easy to turn into makeshift stakes. Like leeches hiding out in a salt factory."

Ethan followed Grady's gaze. "Don't vampires have to be invited into a place?"

"Only private residences. Any place deemed public is a free-for-all, including businesses. Even after hours," Grady answered, grabbing some gear from the floorboard of the back seat.

"Motels? Can they just waltz in your room or does that count as private? What about a bed and breakfast?" Ethan asked with genuine curiosity as Grady handed him some kind of wristband device. He had no clue what the contraption was, but he laced it onto his arm anyway.

"There's my inquisitive boy." Grady seemed genuinely pleased to have his apprentice back. Though, now, Ethan was much more. Grady didn't answer the question.

"I know your powers are greater than any vampire-slaying technology we've created, but if you do need backup, simply press the silver button and aim at your target," Grady instructed. He indicated a small stud on the side of a flat circular surface which was slightly elevated on the wristband. The device resembled a watch without a face.

"What does it do?" Ethan asked, eying the device.

"I'd say to give it a try, but I know your stance on

supernatural eradication and you'd never forgive me," Grady admitted. "It emits a super-concentrated, short-range electromagnetic pulse. Like a small-scale solar flare. Burns them upon impact, but try not to hit any human life with it. Especially me. I'll die someday, but I'd rather not have my demise be by lethal exposure to gamma rays. Magical or otherwise. Oh, and you can only use this once before it needs to be recharged; best to save it for potential life or death situations."

"Shit." Ethan let out a long breath, looking at the device again as though a bomb were now strapped onto his wrist.

"Oh, it's completely safe. Just don't press the button unless you need to," Grady tried to reassure him with a small pat on the forearm. Ethan didn't feel very reassured.

"Whoa. Wait," Ethan interjected. "You're implying magic has the ability to harness, or at least replicate, the properties of radiation and thermodynamics."

"Quite effectively if the mage is skilled enough," Grady answered as if this were all old hat.

Awestruck, Ethan asked, "What about nuclear fusion?"

"Come on," Grady revealed a telling smile but avoided answering. "If they're not already aware we're here, then they will be soon."

"So much for the element of surprise," Ethan said, exiting the car with Grady.

"Oh, believe me. You'll definitely be a surprise for them." Grady beamed at him with so much confidence, Ethan realized his return was more than a lover's homecoming. He could potentially set the balance of Shady Pines right in no time. He was here to be the hero, and that might be what Grady was waiting for all along.

Grady slipped on a pair of leather gloves and pried a few menacing shattered panes of glass out of the window so they would be able to slip inside. The front of the store was dark as the business had recently closed up for the night, but a light shone from the back. Probably the office area, and there was likely still an employee present, which would explain why the security system hadn't been activated yet. Grady hopped through the window with effortless skill, but Ethan clumsily hoisted himself in and hit his knee on a nearby hutch. He winced and sucked in his breath with minor pain.

Grady ignored his klutzy plight and shifted to a guarded position behind an armoire. Ethan hobbled over next to him in the hidden niche and rubbed his knee, hoping the throbbing ache would quickly subside.

The store was far from silent. There were loud sounds from the back as though things were being broken and rifled through. And a shaky female voice was pleading.

"Damn. I suspected they might have a citizen," Grady lamented as he pulled out and loaded his handheld crossbow.

"So, this is now a rescue mission?" Ethan reasoned. He peeked around the side of the armoire in hopes of discerning where the woman's voice was coming from.

The sound was definitely coming from the lighted room in the back.

"Let's just head straight back and ambush the—" Ethan was cut short as a stocky male vampire leaped from the shadows and knocked him back into an un-upholstered settee. The frail woodwork frame cracked beneath their weight, and they tumbled to the ground. Caught by surprise, Ethan hesitated a moment too long, and the vampire lunged toward his neck, fangs bared.

Thwomp. Grady shot one of his stake arrows straight through the vampire's torso from the back. The creature cried out momentarily before going limp. Ethan pushed him onto the floor and looked to Grady appreciatively.

"I thought you could take care of yourself?" Grady teased.

"Just letting you get warmed up." Ethan smirked as he stood in the pile of broken furniture. He rubbed his palms together and concentrated. Feeling confident, a blue glow emitted and encompassed his hands.

"Oh, I'm plenty warmed up. Thank you." Grady smiled precociously.

"Great, because I'm going to need backup," Ethan replied. Their scuffle had been noticed by the other vampires. Three more poured out of the office, locked sights on him, and quickly headed down the main aisle.

Without hesitation, Ethan stepped out of the shadows and strode, fearlessly, straight for them. Two of the vampires slowed their pace but the third, looking ready for a challenge, made an attempt to run for him.

Ethan raised his left hand and let his energy flow out, mingling with and manipulating the natural energy around him, forcing the air to turn into a solid structure like a small shielding wall. The vampire ran headfirst into his shield and fell backward, confused and disoriented. The other two suddenly seemed unsure of continuing their attack.

Ethan didn't give them the chance to decide. With his right hand, he emitted a ball of shimmering starlight that hit one of them square in the face. The creature was dazed for a moment and then crumpled to the floor in slumber. Ethan repeated the move on the remaining vampire with the same result.

Ethan's distraction gave the fallen vampire an opportunity to grapple for him. Yet again, he failed miserably as Grady revealed himself from the shadows to shoot a stake into his chest.

Strolling up beside Ethan, Grady surveyed the two sleeping vampires at their feet.

"That's it? You put them to sleep?" He produced a mildly disappointed frown. "You're like a fairy from a Charles Perrault tale?"

"Wha—no!" Ethan scoffed. "I'm a *sandman*. What did you think I would do?"

Grady simply looked him up and down, mocking judgment, and then spun on his heel and proceeded toward the office in the back of the store.

"I'm *not* a fairy!" Ethan insisted, blushing, as he dutifully followed along behind him.

Whatever remaining vampires waiting within the office were quite aware Grady and Ethan were now standing on the other side of the wall. The door to the office was wide open, light shining out, but the room was abnormally silent, save for a few muffled murmurs, most likely coming from their gagged hostage.

Grady reached into a pocket in his long coat and withdrew a small cylindrical glass vial containing an opalescent liquid. Some extraordinary supernatural concoction, Ethan was sure. Grady raised his left hand and then slowly lifted his index, middle, and ring fingers in turn as he indicated a silent three-count before tossing the vial into the room.

Now the gagging sounds came from different voices, and Ethan definitely smelled the odor of garlic. Grady barged into the office, Ethan following, and quickly assessing the situation. There were two vampires, currently wincing and choking on the tainted air, and a middle-aged woman with fearful brown eyes hunched in the corner of the room.

She looked to the newcomers with surprised relief, but her gaze was instantly drawn to Ethan's glowing hands. Regaining her wits as the vampires were momentarily deterred, she pulled a cell phone out of her jeans pocket and turned the camera on.

"Wait. I wouldn't—" Grady began to dissuade her, but one of the vampires had recovered from the overbearing garlic stench and pounced on him.

Grady, empty-handed at the moment, only grabbed him by the shoulders. He shoved the creature back to keep the monster's fangs at bay.

"Ethan, a little help?" He grunted from the strain.

The second vampire dived at Ethan to prevent his intervention, but Ethan levitated above him and reached to place his palms over the vampire's eyes. The creature dropped to his knees and then toppled face-first into the dingy linoleum floor, fast asleep. Ethan set back on the ground, his entire body illuminated electric blue, as he turned to face Grady and his attacker.

"We've had enough of you and your meddling shit!" The remaining vampire growled at Grady. The creature overpowered Grady by grabbing his right arm and twisting his wrist back with a crack.

Grady cried out with searing agony as the vampire sank his fangs into his neck.

Ethan jumped onto the creature's back and wrapped his electrified body around him. He'd thought of using the device on his wrist, but there was little time, and he wasn't sure he'd be able to manage to aim without also hitting Grady.

The maneuver worked and the vampire released Grady, who backed into the wall as he grasped his mangled wrist.

The creature struggled to free himself from Ethan's hold, but the intense flow of energy was too much for him to fight and he flailed aimlessly.

Ethan was high on his own power and enraged that the vampire had almost succeeded in killing Grady. Instead of putting him to sleep, he used a free hand to reach into his own jacket pocket, pulling out something a little more old-fashioned.

"I'm a pretty open-minded guy," Ethan said, hanging on as the vampire tried to toss him off. "But nobody fucks with my boyfriend."

Ethan put the vampire in a chokehold and wrapped his free hand around to stab him in the chest with a wooden stake. He hopped off backward, levitating for a moment as the vampire went down.

The glow around Ethan flickered and dimmed as he landed on his feet again. Or was the poor lighting just from the room? The electricity in the office mimicked this unstable flow. The lights shuttered off and on repeatedly until they felt like they were inside a giant zoetrope.

In the quick pauses of darkness, Ethan swore a dark-hooded figure appeared next to him. His surroundings began to interchange between the office and a strange forest. He recognized the wooded area of the Dream World. Frantically, he began to worry he'd somehow gone into a self-inflicted sleep trance.

With each flicker, the disguised creature appeared closer until they were face-to-face; although, there was no face to be seen. Only a black void, inside a dark cloak with glimmering green eyes hidden within. There was something familiar in the thing's eyes that he couldn't quite place.

The mysterious figure stood before him, assessing him. Then, without a word, the entity gave a sweep of its black-as-night cloak and retreated to the woods.

Suddenly, Ethan was back in the office again. The trees had disappeared and the figure was nowhere in sight. His energy flared back up, and the lights in the room stabilized and remained on.

Amazed, Grady looked to Ethan, between pained grimaces. He'd actually done it. Ethan had killed someone. Well, some*thing*, anyway. And now that he had, Grady wasn't entirely sure how he felt. The sickening heaviness of guilt rose within. The more time Ethan spent with him, the more his innocence surely slipped away.

The realization that Ethan would kill to save him was a hollow victory. Would he have done the same if he didn't have someone he loved to protect, or would he have simply continued to put every creature into a peaceful slumber? A line had been crossed. One even Grady didn't have anymore. And now he wondered how long that line would remain visible for Ethan as well. Was this the result of his influence? Had he single-handedly corrupted the one brilliant ray of light their world had left?

You fine-tuned him into another disposable supernatural weapon for your arsenal. Marcus's words rang clear in his mind.

His inner turmoil was halted, however, as a digital beep echoed in the room.

Grady and Ethan both turned to the woman huddled in the corner. A woman who had just recorded the most fascinating footage to ever be caught on camera.

Eight: Exposed

"WE'RE NOT GOING to hurt you, but please, hand over the phone." Ethan used his best diplomatic efforts to try to coax the unsettled woman. She was clearly terrified and clinging desperately to the device as if the tiny object were a life preserver.

"No way." She shook her head defiantly, prompting her chin-length, shaggy black hair to whisk around wildly. She steadfastly held her ground, though she was still huddled up against the wall, and her almond eyes gave away her fear.

"Please? You have no idea what you've just recorded," Ethan insisted as he slowly approached her with his hand out.

"Yes, I do. Evidence. No one will ever believe me otherwise!" she replied.

"What did those guys want with you?" Ethan questioned, switching tactics and hoping to elicit both some answers and some trust.

"I don't know. They said they were looking for the Collector," she offered shakily. "I have no idea who they were talking about, though."

"A collector of what?" Ethan pressed.

"Furniture?" The woman gestured largely at the storefront, as though that was a ridiculous question. "I have no idea! But we get so many people in who collect antique pieces, I have no way to know who they wanted."

"May I please see your phone?" Ethan tried again, attempting to appear as calm and friendly as possible.

"I said no way, man!" She grasped the device close to her chest.

"Give him the goddamned phone! You've seen what he can do. Don't test his patience," Grady demanded, grunting miserably, through gritted teeth. He was still grasping his injured wrist. Pain was clearly making him impatient.

Ethan grimaced at him for suggesting he'd ever be so cruel, even if his threat was only a ruse.

"He said he wouldn't hurt me." She attempted to argue, but Grady's cross expression persuaded her to reluctantly hand the phone over to Ethan.

"They'll never believe me now," she lamented.

"Yes, they will." Ethan groaned, holding the phone up, screen facing Grady. "She was posting a live video."

"Oh, for fuck's sake. I hate social media!" Grady snapped.

Ethan deleted the video and pocketed her phone.

"Wait. You can't keep that!" she protested.

Ethan knelt in front of her and gently held his palms to her temples, in turn, causing her to fall fast asleep. A cool blue wave of energy transferred from his fingertips into her skull. After a moment, he stood back as she remained sleeping.

"What was that? What did you do?" Grady's curiosity piqued. Still wincing through his own discomfort, he walked over to inspect the slumbering middle-aged woman's form.

"I altered her memory," Ethan explained. "I gave her a dream. I replaced her memory with a dream of being robbed by some average run-of-the-mill thugs. Basically, she'll remember the dream as reality and what happened will feel like a vague nightmare she had while she was unconscious. The thugs stole her phone and knocked her out."

"Hmm. Not much of a lie really," Grady said.

They turned to assess the sleeping vampires, but they'd all disappeared.

"Dammit! They must've fled when the lights went haywire," Grady cursed.

"I'm sure we'll see them again." Ethan wasn't particularly thrilled by the prospect.

"I'm sure you're right. Let's take the phone back to Chris to see if he can find a way to eradicate that video's existence. I wish the solution were as simple as pressing delete," Grady said. "It'll find a way to haunt us, and we've got enough ghosts showing up on a regular basis already. I hope you don't mind driving."

Ethan took a look at Grady's broken wrist and cringed.

"Can you fix it? With magic?" he asked hopefully.

"I'm not Vivian," Grady bemoaned. "And she's not taking my calls. She's been a rather inefficient friend lately, I must say." He attempted to jest. "I have some remedies a shaman once gave me I can take for the pain, instead of recreation for once, but I'm definitely on human time when it comes to the healing process."

Careful to avoid his injury, Ethan gave him a tight hug and a relieved kiss, thankful they were both still alive.

"YOU BROKE MY Grady?" Chris exclaimed in an overdramatic way as he took a look at Grady's wrist. "He went three months fighting vampires alone with barely a scrape—mostly thanks to my help, of course. One day alongside you and now he's irrevocably handicapped."

"I'm fine." Grady rolled his eyes. He'd drunk a helpful elixir in the car on their drive back, so the pain must have subsided a bit, "Or at least I will be."

"Nope. You're lame. Completely useless to us now. We'll have to put you down. Ship you off to the demon hunter glue factory," Chris teased with a straight face. Then, completely serious, he turned to Ethan. "Why didn't you use my death ray?"

Ethan had been actively and, unsuccessfully, trying to come up with something clever to say in defense of Grady's injury, but Chris was a conversational bullet train who didn't seem capable of making stops. "Your what?"

Chris tapped the device on Ethan's wrist. "Dude, you obviously need weapons training. Tesla and Marconi would be so disappointed."

"I handled everything just fine without your gadgets. Some of us are naturally powerful," Ethan remarked bitterly. He unhooked the device and shoved it across the countertop. Grady's eyebrows flew up in slight surprise at his iciness.

"Where's my mom?" Ethan inquired crossly. Holding his ground against this guy shouldn't be so hard. He'd blasted him across the room earlier in the evening, yet for whatever reason, Chris still made Ethan feel like a petulant child.

Childish or not, the question was valid enough to catch him off guard. Karen wasn't anywhere in sight, and Chris had not-so-inconspicuously rushed into the front lobby moments after they'd arrived; no longer wearing his jacket but donning an orange muscle shirt instead. His styled blue hair had clearly been mussed and tampered with.

"She um… She'll just be—" Chris fumbled. For once, he was at a loss for words. Chris glanced over his shoulder, down the hallway from where he'd appeared, and turned back to Ethan with an overcompensating grin. "Restroom. She had to use the restroom. Should be out in a sec."

Ethan glared at him but dropped the issue. He didn't actually want details. He only hoped his mother had enough sense to have her clothes back on once she decided to rejoin them. So much for hoping nothing romantic was going on. He wondered if his mother had somehow been possessed, in his absence. He narrowed his eyes judgmentally at Chris. *That has to be what's going on. She's totally possessed. Out of her mind. He probably cast a love spell on her*, he decided spitefully.

"We've got a project for you," Grady interjected, setting them back on track. He nodded at Ethan to produce the phone.

Ethan fished the device out of his pocket and dropped the phone on the counter. He didn't feel like handing anything directly over to Chris. Too much risk of making skin contact, and he decided Chris had already had enough "contact" with the Roam family for one night.

As if on cue, Karen appeared from the hallway. Thankfully, fully dressed. But her hair was brushed up into a messy ponytail, a telltale sign of being in a rush to make herself presentable.

As Ethan's cheeks grew hotter, his anger caused him to levitate slightly. He quickly suppressed his emotions as best he could and planted his sneakers firmly back on the floor.

No one noticed, as they were focused on Chris and the phone. Except for Benny, who had loped back inside, in werehuahua form, through a small doggy door in the back of the building. He was now excitedly running circles around Ethan's legs.

Ethan bent and scooped him into his arms as he would any pet he felt affection for and laughed as Benny energetically wiggled around, licking his neck and chin.

"Stop, man. That's so weird," Ethan giggled. At least his antics helped lighten his mood, which might have been the point, as Benny calmed and rested casually in his arms with self-satisfaction. Ethan scratched him lightly behind the ear.

"What's going on?" Karen asked. She leaned against the edge of the desk, where Chris had already set the phone on a small rectangular crystal plate.

"Unfortunately, Ethan's supernatural prowess has been exposed to the general populace," Grady revealed with a frown. "He was filmed in action. We've deleted the recording, but we have no idea how many viewers might have seen the video. I'm concerned the footage definitely exists on a server, or cloud, or whatnot."

"Is 'whatnot' the extent of your familiarity with modern technology? You seriously have no idea how this works, do you?" Chris smirked. Then he pulled out a small silver rod, the size of an ink pen, which emitted a purple ball of light from the end, and slowly traced the length of the phone.

"Is that your magic wand?" Ethan commented with snark.

Chris simply smiled, letting him have the dig. It was only fair.

"The practical implications of modern technology is all whatnot and hullabaloo so far as I'm concerned," Grady lectured with distinct pretension. "I find people, as a whole, underwhelming in their lack of capacity to engage their imaginations with scientific progress. You open them up to endless possibilities, and all they want to do is post prank videos, read celebrity gossip, and take pictures of ducks' faces."

"I think you mean 'duck face,' Karen corrected with an amused snort.

"That's what I said," Grady deadpanned.

"Yeah, well, lofty expectations of your average Joe aside, I think you joining the rest of us in the digital world might be way past due," Chris remarked, still scanning the phone. "So says your 'Kolchak' system of organizing case files," he added, gesturing with his elbow at the metal filing cabinets filled with disheveled manila folders behind them.

"That's why I hired you. You're as close to involved with the digital world as I wish to be," Grady remarked simply. He then scrutinized Chris's work. "What exactly are you doing?"

"Firstly, 'hired' implies monetary compensation. I do this as a favor. Secondly, it's 'digital stuff.' Nothing you'd be interested in," Chris teased.

Grady rolled his eyes and faked a sigh. He'd walked right into that one.

Ethan held back a grin. Not many sparred well in a battle of wits with Grady. Maybe Chris would win him over, after all. Maybe.

"I'm practically paying you," Grady reminded him. "You've spent a fortune on takeout since you arrived."

"Which reminds me. Pizza is in the break room. Just running a quick diagnostic analysis. Basic stuff," Chris answered. "So, the good news is I can totally wipe away any traces of footage from everywhere it made its way to. The bad news is the video was seen by twenty-six unique viewers. Not very many in the grand scheme of things, but if I know anything to do with grand schemes, it's that the smallest things are always what make the biggest difference. I can't take away those people's memories. That's beyond my ability. And we have no real way to discern what any of them might do with the knowledge they now possess, even if they have no proof. For now, there's nothing more than a shared hallucination."

"For now," Grady repeated, lost in a deep, serious thought. The index finger of his healthy hand rested across his lips; his injured arm rested on the counter.

"Someone other than you was bound to find him, eventually," Chris stated, directing the comment only to Grady. He then worked his magic on the phone to eradicate the existence of the video completely.

"This...this is why I hate technology. It exposes everything sacred to those least worthy of knowing," Grady sighed.

Ethan stole a glance at his mom, who looked confused and worried.

He carefully set Benny back down and the little dog whined, sensing something was wrong.

Ethan caught Grady staring at him with doting concern and consideration. He'd seen that look before. Right before his world was turned upside down and inside out last Halloween.

"What is it?" Ethan wished he didn't have to ask. He knew whatever Grady was thinking wouldn't be anything he wanted to hear, and the night had already proven exhausting enough.

"You have to tell him. The secret is out now. It's time," Chris softly prompted Grady as he set the—now least of their worries—phone aside. He crossed his arms in firm resolve. "His life depends on it."

Nine: Hunted

"MY LIFE BEING dependent on information everyone else is privy to except for me is starting to become a really disconcerting trend. Just FYI," Ethan grumbled. Honestly, his life was always in danger these days, so this news, whatever it was, was beginning to feel like another drop in the bucket.

"Not everyone," Karen corrected her son. She shot Chris a disapproving look, indicating she was also out-of-the-loop.

"Ethan, I promise this isn't something I was actively hiding from you," Grady prefaced his defense before any accusations were made. "It hadn't been pertinent to bring the matter up; you've just come back, and there was no immediate threat. And the whole situation is really more of Chris's territory."

"Man! My shoulders sure are sore from the weight you thrust on them," Chris frowned, only half joking.

"Honestly, no surprise there." Ethan sighed. "You like to keep fatal secrets from your boyfriends. I get it. It's sort of your *thing*."

"That's a bit harsh," Grady remarked. After being hit with the low blow, he pursed his lips.

"Sounds like some weird kink," Chris remarked as he casually opened a container of orange Tic Tacs and poured them in his mouth. Ethan began to suspect he was a stress eater.

"Excuse me! Mom present!" Karen reminded them. She waved her hands in front of her face and shook her head, as though hoping to dispel any traumatizing thoughts.

Good. Now she knows how unpleasant that feels, Ethan thought smugly.

"Frankly, I'd be more concerned with the fact your son used his powers to kill someone tonight. That's going to draw a lot of attention, and I don't mean only from a short-lived video," Chris advised.

"What!" Karen whipped her attention back to Ethan. He'd never seen her look so hurt before. At least, not with him being the cause.

"Clarification." Ethan held up his hands, trying to halt the train wreck he felt barreling toward him. "He attacked Grady. I had to do *something*. And—and he was a vampire."

"Species shouldn't matter," Chris remarked, finishing off his Tic Tacs. "Specifically, not to *you*."

"What's that supposed to mean? And it doesn't," Ethan admitted, not wanting to be mistaken for any form of bigot or speciesist. "He could have been anyone. He was trying to kill Grady, and that's all that mattered in the moment. I just...reacted."

"Yeah, that's the worrisome part... Look, I guess this is as good a place to start as any," Chris sighed, becoming uncharacteristically serious.

Ethan noticed Grady had walked away to lock up the office and switch the sign in the window to "Closed." He turned off the lights in the waiting area, as well, before rejoining the group at Chris's makeshift work station behind the front desk.

"Rewinding to 'unwanted attention,' tell me something," Chris started. "When you killed the vampire, did you see Death?"

"Well, yeah. I killed someone," Ethan awkwardly answered.

"No." Chris gave a small huff but remained patient. "I mean, Death. Like the actual guy. Did you see him? You know, black robes, skeleton hands, etc.?"

A chill ran down Ethan's spine as he recalled the ghostly apparition who had confronted him.

"I might have…" Ethan was reluctant to believe what he'd seen had actually been such an archetypal being. "I mean, I thought—for a moment—that I saw *someone*. I don't remember any skeleton hands, though. "

"Did he have a scythe?" Chris was overly enthusiastic at the prospect.

"No," Ethan answered. He thought back carefully. "He wasn't carrying anything."

"Damn." Chris frowned. "Too bad. A scythe would have been a dead giveaway. Ha! Puns."

"Why does it matter what I did or didn't see?" Ethan asked in frustration.

"Killing shouldn't be in your nature," Chris began to explain. "At least, not the supernatural side. *Somnium viators*—sandmen—aren't typically killers. Not in any predatory or emotionally based way. Not even for self-preservation and definitely not as a crime of passion. There *are* predators who can manipulate dreams, but they can't travel the subconscious mind to alternate dimensions. They certainly can't create tangible portals to those places in our reality. Those gifts belonged to the original Sandman and were passed down through his lineage. He was believed to be a sort of demigod. An impartial being of light who helped keep the balance of good and evil in the interdimensional subconscious. His descendants, the sandmen, are supposed to be extremely docile creatures. Which is a major reason why you're almost extinct."

"We put people to sleep. We don't kill them…" Ethan reasoned, self-consciously crossing his arms. He put the pieces together. "It was easy for others to manipulate and command us if we had no way or will to fight back."

"Or worse. Eradicate you," Chris solemnly revised the statement. "The jury is still out on whether or not this is true, but some believed the Sandman's arrival to our plane is what brought supernatural creatures here in the first place. Creatures more powerful than us, who seek to kill us, much of the time purely for their own amusement. Those people did everything they could to try to rid the Earth of any potential paranormal newcomers, if you get my drift."

Ethan felt a surge of sadness and anger within him at the thought of the many terrors his ancestors must have faced. They'd all been wiped out at this point. He suspected even his own father had possibly met a similar fate; though, he hoped with his entire being that wasn't the case.

"Right. I'm on the endangered species list," Ethan concurred with a concerned look at his mother. She didn't seem to be taking any of this in stride. Her eyes conveyed a dark emptiness which let him know she was thinking of his father. He knew she must have the same fears.

"Grady's worried you might meet a similar fate," Chris revealed.

Grady began to protest, but Chris plowed forward in spite of him.

"But now...I don't think we need to worry so much. However, it's still better for you to be informed," he said.

"Why would we not worry?" Karen practically gasped at Chris's casual dismissal of doom.

"Because Ethan here, unlike his predecessors, clearly has the fluke of free will," Chris explained as though the variable should be obvious. "Don't take this as an insult, but I think the sandman side of your genetics has been watered down. You have passion. You can fight. You can kill. You've evolved. But without performing some experiments, I couldn't tell you why."

"And *that* is precisely the danger I *am* concerned about," Grady interjected. He was speaking directly to Ethan but cast a sideways glance at Chris. "There are those who might seek you out purely to entrap you, to study you, and to use you. And I mean that in the crudest and most inhumane of ways. A group of men who have existed as long as supernaturals have walked the Earth and whose motives and justifications are as dark and morbid as the creatures they claim to have dominion over."

Karen reached for Ethan's hand. He gripped hers in his; more so to calm her nerves than his own. Everyone wanted to capture or kill him these days; he wasn't as fazed by the news as they had expected him to be. If anything, he was suspicious.

"How do you know so much?" Ethan inquired as he narrowed his eyes at Chris. Could a techno-mage have somehow gleaned all this knowledge from the uncharted corners of the internet? He doubted this was the sort of information anyone would ever save in a hackable format.

Chris hesitated. He seemed to be mulling over the possible ramifications of revealing the truth.

Taking a deep breath, he stated, "Because I used to be one of them. A Hunter. And...so was your father."

Ten: The Order of Azoth

"YOU KNEW VINCENT?"

"You knew my dad?"

Karen's voice trampled over Ethan's as they reacted in unison. She with hurt accusation and he with eager exuberance.

"No, sorry," Chris quickly modified. "I can see how that came across wrong. I never met the guy. I knew *of* him. What I meant was we were both inducted in the HOA."

"The Home Owner's Association?" Ethan was bewildered.

"The Hunters of the Order of Azoth," Grady explained, cutting to the chase. "One of the oldest and most dangerous secret societies that exist. The Order of Azoth was founded around the third century by an elite group of alchemists and continues to function to this day. In order to stay hidden, their numbers are small, but their members are nonpareil in their skills and talents. I was invited to join, but I turned them down," he added smugly.

"With some help from yours truly. And we both lived to tell the tale. Which is impressive in its own right," Chris admitted, verbally patting both of them on the back. Grady seemed mutually pleased.

"So, what? What does that mean? Some ancient cult of old wizards is hunting me to slice and dice me for their creepy rituals? Is that what you're saying?" Ethan attempted to sort the information, unsure at what level of concern he should be functioning.

"Oh, no," Chris clarified. "The high alchemists never do the grunt work. That's what the Hunters are for. Some are highly skilled mages, but a lot of them are regular men and women who are proficient at tracking, capturing and/or killing things. Former soldiers, assassins, martial arts experts, even notorious poachers. The Order of Azoth not only studies the supernatural creatures of the world but they're also self-proclaimed balance keepers. The problem is they're not balanced at all. The scales tend to tip in their favor toward their end goals. They cull the herds, if you will. Like most hunters, they justify their actions on the idea of keeping a population's numbers in check."

"So, basically they're supernatural hit men. Great. Then why don't they do something about all the vampires?" Ethan asked. "Seems like they're more of a problem than I ever would be. There's only one of me."

"Incorrect! Well, not the one of you part but the assumption that you'd be less of a threat. You see, vampires are low-level concerns. Class Three entities at best," Chris answered. "You're a Class Five. Which is…well, pretty fucking amazing. A Class Five is essentially the holy grail to these alchemists; forgive the religiously divisive bon mot. A creature that isn't bound to Earth or the spirit plane—ghost dimension, if you will. Class Fives can exist in multiple dimensions or have the ability to travel across parallel universes at will. There are only three Class Fives we know for certain exist: Sandman, Death, and Mercury. Most HOA members never meet a Class Five in their entire lifetime, although that's the ultimate goal. The Order exists for the express purpose of—"

"Slow down," Karen interrupted, rubbing her temples. "I can't believe Vincent would ever be a part of something like this. And you are too?"

She then glared at Grady. "You let him into our lives. Why would you bring him here? To us? To my son!"

Chris fell inordinately silent.

"For protection!" Grady defended his friend. "Chris isn't a member anymore. They think he's dead. And he's our best line of defense against them. You won't meet anyone else who has the intel or the abilities he does. They can't track him, and so long as we stay vigilant, then they won't be able to track Ethan either. Or, at least, they shouldn't have been until that blasted video was uploaded. Now I've no idea how much time we have before they show up."

Benny whimpered.

"I'm sorry, Karen." Chris's apology sounded sincere. Karen seemed to accept it, but she still looked unsettled.

"But what was Vincent's role in this?" she pressed. "It doesn't sound like him at all. He wouldn't support such a horrible group."

"Did these guys kill my dad?" Ethan asked. The possibility seemed the most obvious answer. Perhaps his father had tried to leave them like Chris did, or reject them as Grady had, but for whatever reason, he hadn't been as lucky in his escape.

"No," Chris answered, producing an uneasy frown. "I only know this because I was a high clearance agent and had orders to engage a Class Five if I ever met one in the field—which I never did. Your father worked alongside the Order. He thought he was helping to make the world a safer place by transporting supernaturals out. In return, he had the Order's oath of protection. What he didn't know was they would've protected him, regardless. Their goal was to keep him around. Keep tabs on him. Which they effectively did through branding him. They needed him. They don't want to kill sandmen. They want to control them."

Chris turned around and pulled up his shirt to show them a scar on the back of his neck. The injury indicated his flesh had been burned off at some point.

"The mark of Azoth," he explained before pulling his shirt back down and facing them again. "Their way of tracking their members. The mark only stops working if you die, or if the image is burned off, and it alerts them when either event has happened. I staged my death by fire. They were never alerted about Vincent. They didn't kill your dad. I know that much. They wanted him alive. And, somehow, they had no clue you existed. He did a great job hiding the fact he was even married. Double life extraordinaire. I wouldn't be surprised if he'd eventually found a way to hide."

"So what do they think happened to him?" Ethan asked, hoping to get the one answer he wanted more than anything else in the world.

"No idea," Chris replied in a flat tone. "He disappeared. Blip. Gone. Never came back."

"He escaped," Ethan realized. "He traveled. To save himself. No one would be able to get to him if he traveled to a place they couldn't track. But...that means he abandoned us."

Ethan was crushed. His entire life he'd lamented the fact he'd grown up without a father. He'd shed so many tears over the unfairness of his death. Now, that fate felt preferable to the reality that his dad was potentially nothing more than a self-centered supernatural coward.

"He wouldn't do that. He wouldn't leave Ethan behind. Vulnerable to the same men," Karen defended.

"How do you know?" Ethan shot back with a sudden flash of anger. "It's not like you ever truly knew him! Not the *real* him. He lied to you, Mom! He lied to everyone...everyone except Arthur, and even he has no idea what really happened. Or so he says... Face it. He left! He left and he didn't take us with him."

"Whoa there, Quick Draw," Chris intervened on Karen's behalf. "I'm not here to slander your dad. In fact, I agree with Karen."

"What?" Ethan turned to him with intense watery eyes. He looked like he might like to blast the entire office building apart with his energy. Grady rested a comforting hand on his shoulder.

"Your dad had no clue the Order was up to anything nefarious. He thought they were the good guys. He thought they were saving people. There was nothing to escape from, as far as he would've known," Chris explained. "Unless...somebody knew the truth and got to him under the radar. But that's extremely unlikely. The Order had him on a tight leash and with limited intel. If you ask me, there *was* foul play but, I'm sorry, no one ever found any answers to the mysterious disappearance of Vincent Roam."

"And now this group might be after my son?" Karen reiterated with worry. "Because of this video."

"Nah, I think we're safe. The chances of any of those viewers having ties to the Order are slim to none," Chris assessed. He handed the phone back over to Ethan to do with as he pleased. "But I'd try to keep the exercise of your powers off the grid for a while if at all possible. As a precaution. If I can pick you up on my radar that heavily then so can they. Turns out your power is like an atomic bomb going off. Hard to miss," he advised.

"How are we supposed to deal with all of these vampires if Grady is injured and my hands are tied?" Ethan pressed as he reigned in his emotions, pocketing the phone.

"We'll figure something out," Grady said without elaborating.

"I'm not trying to make things more difficult," Chris expressed. "You're a smart kid—"

"I'm not a kid," Ethan interjected with an overt annoyance that was becoming far too familiar a response to Chris.

"Look," Chris sighed, and Ethan noted the slight agitation in his voice. "Energy can't be created or destroyed, right? So, every time you use your powers, that energy comes from somewhere. Specifically, it's harnessed from surrounding latent psi energy, universal chi, and funneled through a conduit, i.e., you. Believe me. Mages are going to start noticing those energy spikes. Especially if they're nosing around in the right places."

Ethan saw he had no choice but to concede the matter. He was overwhelmed enough, and Chris was actually making sense, which frustrated him.

"Fine. Okay. I'll lay off the sandman tricks for now," Ethan acquiesced due to emotional exhaustion. "Hopefully, you're right, and nothing bad will come from this. Grady and I can work on a different plan of attack tonight and we'll regroup tomorrow evening. I feel like I need a break...from everything. At least for the next twenty-four hours."

"No one gets a break from life until they're dead. Sometimes not even then. But I hear you. I'll pull an all-nighter to keep watch on our surveillance setups around town. Make sure we're in the clear." Chris said, taking initiative.

"Thank you," Grady nodded.

Chris looked to Karen.

"Oh, I'm staying," Karen assured with a stern tone. "If people are after my son, then I'm definitely going to monitor that situation. Plus, I still have a few more personal questions for you on all of this Order business."

"That's fair," Chris said.

Grady gently squeezed Ethan's shoulder with his good hand, "Care to drive us home?"

"Yeah, let's go." Ethan fished the car keys out of his pocket. "You have more of your own explaining to do, by the way."

"The interrogations never cease," Grady sighed, but the quip was in good humor.

"I think you'll find my methods of extracting information *very* effective." Ethan smirked seductively as their eyes met.

"But no sandman tricks!" Chris chimed in as a teasing reminder. Karen palmed her face and shook her head, most likely trying to dispel any thoughts of her son's intimate personal affairs.

"No sandman tricks," Ethan playfully repeated like a vow. He offered Chris a small smile as they left. A gesture of team unity. With things as crazy as they were, he knew they had to at least attempt to get along.

THERE WASN'T ANY trouble on their surveillance for the rest of the night.

Karen allowed Chris to plead his case for forgiveness.

Ethan and Grady found familiar comfort in each other's embrace. Lips to skin and bodies entwined. A few sandman tricks may have been employed, after all, but only minor ones to dispel the pain in Grady's hand.

They were able to enjoy a restful slumber in one another's arms.

Up to this point, they had been wary of the monsters plaguing the night. No one had expected evil would present itself boldly and by daylight.

Nor that Ethan would befriend it.

Eleven: The Sandman & the Vampire

GRADY LIGHTLY RAN his fingers through Ethan's disheveled black hair. He was still curled up against him, head resting on his chest and arm wrapped around his waist. He was breathing evenly so Grady assumed he must still be asleep.

With Ethan snuggled and relaxed beside him, he felt at peace for the first time in ages. He'd nearly forgotten they had any cares in the world. However, his injured wrist quickly reminded him, and he released a small grunt of discomfort as he tangled his fingers in a strand of Ethan's hair. He knew he'd need to take something for the pain again soon. But he didn't mind waiting. He'd endure any pain he had to in order to savor as many moments entwined with Ethan as he could.

They'd been able to realign and mend his wrist themselves, but he thought he'd attempt to contact Vivian again later in the day. A fairly adept witch, she knew how to concoct potions able to heal most non-fatal injuries. Hopefully, she could put the past behind her enough to help him out. He didn't want to have to visit an actual doctor. Too much paperwork involved, which was quite undesirable for someone who spent a vast amount of time cleaning up traces of his own existence.

"Mercury," Ethan mumbled lightly. Grady wasn't sure if he had woken or if he was talking in his sleep.

"Hmm?" Grady quietly prompted. He slowly and gently ran his fingertips down Ethan's shoulder and along his arm with a tender caress to rouse him.

"Chris said there were three of us," Ethan spoke up. Clearly, he'd not been sleeping but rather had been immersed in thought.

Ethan lifted his head and rolled onto his stomach in order to face Grady. His expression was one of extreme analysis.

"Death, me, and Mercury," he continued. "Does he mean, like, the Roman god? I thought real deities didn't exist. And if they do, then why only Mercury? Why wouldn't the Order acknowledge more? And who is Azoth anyway?"

"How long have you been awake?" Grady struggled to pull his own thoughts into as sharp a state as his lover's, but he was still groggy and hadn't had any caffeine yet. He rubbed his eyes in an effort to focus.

"Long enough," Ethan admitted. He offered a kittenish smile. "I watched your dreams."

"Of course you did." Grady chuckled lightly. He was equally embarrassed and aroused by the idea.

Grady pushed himself up against his pillow into a slightly more elevated position. Ethan joined him, sitting up beside him under the cream-colored silk covers.

"I don't know much concerning the Order. My personal experience with them is extremely limited," Grady admitted, trying to catch up with Ethan's early morning thoughts. "That's why I wanted Chris to tell you. Azoth isn't a person or a creature, though. I do know that. Azoth is a divine energy. Or so their alchemists believe. *Spiritus animatus.* The universal life force."

"And Mercury? Do you know about him?" Ethan pressed.

"That's the peculiar part," Grady confessed. His brow creased with disappointment at his own lack of information. "You see, traditionally alchemists referred to the element mercury as Azoth. I suppose they found their theory incorrect...but that doesn't explain why they'd now consider Mercury as a living entity. I don't want to make assumptions. I made a mental note to ask Chris more about the matter this evening. I believe there's a lot he has yet to tell either of us. Another one of the many things on my never-ending to-do list. When the only thing I want *to do* is stay put right here, in this bed, with you."

Ethan smiled flirtatiously and shifted himself onto Grady's lap, straddling him. He leaned forward to kiss him with mad devotion. Grady wrapped his good arm around Ethan and pulled him in closer as the warm, soft, texture of their tongues met.

"One day..." Ethan whispered between short, deep kisses. "I'll take us away...from all of this...forever. And we...can just be...alone."

Grady gripped him tighter, indicating his impassioned desire for such a future. But just as he began to lose himself in the moment, Ethan pulled back from their embrace.

"I was thinking," he started with a hopeful tone.

"No." Grady smirked libidinously. "It isn't fair to ask for things when you know I'm not in a position to refuse them. I'll agree to anything right now."

Ethan laughed and pulled Grady's hand from behind his back to hold onto, pressing their palms together. "How do you know I was even going to ask for anything?"

When Ethan bit his lower lip coquettishly, Grady knew he was helpless to his wiles.

"You have the look of a man who knows his strengths and his opponent's weaknesses. That's how," Grady stated. He chuckled lightly. "Out with it, then. What price must I pay for another kiss from my starlit prince?"

"I was going to ask that today before we get wrapped up in vampire hunting and Azoth dodging, we do something special together. Something *normal*. Something we haven't actually done yet," Ethan expressed optimistically. "Officially."

"It's a bit early in the relationship to bring toys into the bed, don't you think? Although, I do have some if you're dead set on experimenting," Grady joked. At least, it was a joke unless Ethan agreed.

"I was going to say we should go out for lunch," Ethan revealed. "Somewhere nice. Just the two of us. An actual official date. Which we haven't actually, officially had yet."

Grady realized he was right. Everything had transpired so quickly between them, and through so much circumstance and tragedy, they'd completely skipped over the whole routine of dating. A matter that didn't bother Grady. He didn't need traditional courtship. He'd be as happy having breakfast in bed with Ethan or walking hand in hand through the garden behind his estate. He felt more value in quiet intimacy.

But he knew the experience was important to Ethan, and he completely understood why. He was Ethan's first. His first kiss. His first love. His first everything. And he'd never even taken him out to lunch.

"Of course," Grady immediately agreed. "Absolutely. We'll go to—no! Dammit."

"What?" Ethan's pleased expression crumpled as Grady's face contorted with frustration.

Grady sighed heavily and looked to the ceiling for forgiveness. "I promised Edwin I'd have lunch with him today. You could go with us, though, if you'd like."

"A date with your dad as the third wheel? Um...no thanks." Ethan rolled his eyes and slid off Grady's lap back onto his own side of the bed.

"I'll put him off." Grady attempted to reel the situation back. "He can wait another day."

"It's fine. Like Chris said, you don't get a break from life," Ethan insisted, crawling out of bed. His clothes were still on the floor from the night before, and he began to pull them on, much to Grady's dismay.

"Ethan, I'm sorry," Grady offered. "That was a stupid response. Of course, I can reschedule with him. He's waited this long, he can wait another day."

"I said it's okay. You need to deal with him. You can't avoid him forever." Ethan turned to him as he zipped up his jeans. Grady's heart sank, taking that as the signal that the matter was closed. He let his head loll back against the headboard as he inwardly cursed himself.

Ethan offered what he probably hoped was a forgiving smile, but Grady knew the situation was much worse. He was disappointed.

"I promise. I'll make this up to you," Grady vowed. "I'll clear my entire schedule tomorrow, just for us. We'll go to lunch, to the riverwalk, shopping, whatever your heart desires. We'll do it. As a couple."

"Sounds great." Ethan nodded as he pulled on his plain black T-shirt, but Grady saw the doubt in his eyes. The truth of the matter was neither of them knew how many more "tomorrows" they had together.

Before he had a chance to offer any more consolations, Ethan said, "I've got things I need to do, anyway. I'm going to run by Arthur's and attempt a friendly interrogation about dream traveler stuff and my dad. Maybe hit up the attic at my mom's house and go through some of his old keepsakes and journals. There might be a clue or something. Maybe I can try to get in contact with Vivian for you. She'll probably answer my call before she would yours."

"That would be great. Thank you," Grady said, trying not to let the regret of his actions show.

"All right." Ethan shoved his hands into his pockets. "I'm going to head out then. I'll see you later."

"Later," Grady echoed, as Ethan headed for the door. "Ethan—"

Ethan stopped and looked back over his shoulder as he rested his hand on the doorknob.

"I do love you," Grady stated genuinely.

"I love you too," Ethan replied, keeping his tone even. He pulled the door shut behind him.

Grady slumped into the bed in defeat, pinching the bridge of his nose with vexation.

"You're an idiot, Alexander. Bloody hell..." he admonished himself, employing his real name for added effect. "Don't let yourself lose him. Not another one. Not this time."

ETHAN TOOK A mellowing sip of his caramel latte as he left the cafe. The partially cloudy morning had brought a crisp chill, but the warmth of his drink counteracted the cool air nicely. Plus, he'd opted for one of his old, plain blue, hooded jackets, instead of the black leather he'd been wearing. He thought it might provide more warmth, but now he considered maybe he just wanted to have a bit of his old self back.

Not that he didn't love, or even sometimes revel, in the fact he was essentially a divine being. His new identity was a vast change from what he'd considered himself before: a nobody. And certainly he was happy to have Grady in his life, even if he was a little miffed at him at the moment. Overall, though, being special meant he never had a moment when he wasn't, well...special. A part of him was longing for the forgotten safety net of anonymity he'd taken for granted and even loathed. Being a nobody had its perks too. No one expected anything from him, and he didn't expect anything from them.

Ethan shuffled down the steps of the cafe toward Grady's car, which he'd borrowed since he knew Grady wouldn't be driving himself anywhere anytime soon. He was about to hop in and head to Arthur's house when he saw a familiar face strolling along the sidewalk across the street.

His short blond curly hair was practically glistening in the sunlight, and he walked with his head held high. He had the demeanor of a dandy prince surveying a kingdom clearly not up to his standards but tolerated out of a pretense of good humor.

The man donned a smart brown plaid button-up overcoat, made up of crisscrossing mocha and sepia-toned stripes. A cobalt blue scarf was fashioned neatly around his neck, and though Ethan couldn't imagine why he'd need anything to keep him warm, he also wore matching brown leather gloves.

He carried on, obliviously wrapped up in thought, without so much as a glance in Ethan's direction.

Spontaneously, Ethan crossed the street, once an opening in traffic allowed, and trotted up beside the man.

"Marcus?" Ethan greeted with surprise.

The vampire, lassoed from his mental musings, turned to see who'd approached him. He smiled pleasantly as he saw his visitor and came to a standstill.

"Ethan," he greeted in return. "What are the odds I'd run into you? Curse of a small town, I suppose. Unless, of course, you've been following me."

"What? No," Ethan assured. He felt nervous and began second-guessing his own resolve to confront the vampire alone. "I was just grabbing a coffee." He held up the paper cup as though a visual illustration were necessary.

"Yes, I can see." Marcus smirked with coy amusement. "I was merely joking. Partially, anyway."

"What are you doing out? In the day? In the sun?" Ethan was a bumbling mess as he immediately dove for answers. Not only had he discovered a vampire doing what a vampire should never be able to do, but something relating to Marcus still caused him to feel bashful and self-conscious.

"Ah, yes." Marcus pretended to be mildly surprised Ethan had noticed the obvious. "I would've figured you'd work that out on your own the moment you saw me, but if you need to be walked through the details, I will graciously supply them."

"Vivian," Ethan responded knowingly. Vivian had given Dacey the ability to walk in daylight. Marcus had said she worked for him. The correlation was obvious.

"Oh, good. You're not as dense as you were starting to look." Marcus produced an approving smile.

"But why would—" Ethan started to ask.

"She imbued me with the gift as a consolation for her involvement in...well, you know," Marcus began obligingly. "You see, she was supposed to be my eyes to watch over him and my hands to steer him when I wasn't around. The whole matter is a story of regrets now. I never should have let him venture out on his own in this world. The lot of you were never worth his time and clearly incapable of doing the one thing I always excelled at. Keeping him safe."

A pang of self-condemnation washed over Ethan. His expression must have been easy to read because Marcus's lofty, cold manner immediately warmed, and Ethan saw something in his eyes he didn't know could even exist there. Sympathy.

"I don't blame *you*," Marcus revealed with a sigh, sounding generous. "You're young and everything is new to you. You've no idea what your mere existence even implies. Dacey wanted to protect you as I always wanted to protect him. He was one of a kind. I feel you are too. Invaluable. And as such, forever a marked man. Not an easy crown to wear. You're the innocent in this. I harbor no grudges against you. The rest of them, I don't have to forgive."

"I'm not innocent, though," Ethan offered. "And I don't actually know I deserve any forgiveness. But I definitely want to earn some."

Marcus let out a small bemused laugh. "Ridiculous. Yearning to earn the favor of a vampire. You *are* young."

Ethan wasn't sure what to say at this juncture, so he awkwardly sipped his latte and shoved his other hand into his jacket pocket. He stared at the cracks in the sidewalk for courage.

"You already have my favor. You're very much like him, you know?" Marcus stated. His voice was uncharacteristically kind, almost longing.

"Like Dacey?" Ethan was taken aback. He couldn't imagine how such a correlation might be made. As far as he knew, they were completely different. Then again, the two vampires had a long history, and Ethan had barely begun to know him. Perhaps there had been more to Dacey than Grady let on.

"I apologize for my behavior last night," Marcus offered, glossing over the acknowledgment of his previous statement. "You caught me at a rare, vulnerable moment. I promise I'm usually more put together."

"It's okay. I understand grief," Ethan tendered kindly. "You seem to be doing a lot better today."

"With conversation, coffee, and the sun, who could not be happy?" Marcus gestured at Ethan's cup, both of them knowing full well he couldn't partake. But Ethan saw, for whatever reason, he was delighted to be in the presence of someone he liked who could. Ethan smiled warmly.

"About Vivian. I don't suppose you've heard from her lately? We've been trying to reach her, but she's ignoring us," Ethan gently prodded. He might as well try to ascertain some information he'd be able to take back to the others from their run-in. He didn't think Grady would be very pleased to hear about Marcus favoring him.

"No, I'm afraid she's left us all in a bind," Marcus revealed. "I'd attempted to call on her yesterday, but it looks as though she's skipped town."

"Damn. Could've really used her help today," Ethan lamented. "Oh well. I guess I understand. We could all use some space from our problems."

Ethan saw nothing but wisdom in him as Marcus chuckled and replied, "Says the man who literally has all the space in the universe. Tell me something, Ethan. If you're so keen to abandon your problems, then why, with a multiverse of options at your fingertips, are you still here in this dreary little speck of dirt town on this boring little planet? What in Byron's name is keeping you here?"

That was a great question. What surprised him was he didn't wrestle to find an answer. It was instantaneous.

"Grady," he provided honestly.

Marcus's expression fell into a mix of disappointment and surprise.

"Ah, yes. The charming Hunter." he pursed his lips. "I'm sure he wouldn't be too thrilled at how much of your time I've taken. I suppose he already forbid you from talking to me. Which, of course, makes you a rebel. I applaud your inherent independent nature, but this marks a good point to bid you good day. I'm sure you, and your coffee, are very busy. And I have no real desire to waste my time in fisticuffs with an Englishman. As therapeutic as that might prove to be."

"You're a lot like him too," Ethan bravely retorted, in reference to Grady, using the vampire's own musing against him.

Marcus paused and Ethan assumed he was deciding if he should take the remark as an insult or a compliment.

"I think I can see all of this a lot more clearly than everyone else." Ethan had finally found his confidence in dealing with the snobbish vampire. Being called inherently independent made everything click. Talking to him, he realized, was similar in a lot of ways to navigating Grady in conversation.

"Oh?" Marcus seemed curious.

"There are no 'bad guys' here. There never were. Only men who cared too much in circumstances which never suited them," Ethan assessed. "And jealously makes monsters out of all men. I won't fall into that. I'm not jealous and I don't think either of you should be. It's a weakness. Not a defense."

"You're an old soul, Ethan." Marcus granted. "I appreciate that."

Ethan wasn't sure why he cared, but Marcus's new esteem for him made him feel empowered. "The truth is I do want to leave and never come back. I mean, maybe only to visit my mom and friends," Ethan opened up. "I don't belong here anymore. But I want to take Grady with me. I just haven't figured out how to do that safely or accurately. But I know there's a way."

Marcus seemed to bite his tongue for a moment before choosing to extend a casual invitation, "*Are* you busy? Would you care to spend the day with me?"

Ethan was stumped. On the one hand, he did have a lot to look into. On the other hand, he'd somehow sparked a friendship with a vampire which might prove fruitful. Marcus seemed to know a lot regarding the people who surrounded Ethan's life and a questionable amount about himself. Maybe he'd be able to interrogate him further on the vampire problem.

"Uh...sure. Yeah. I could do that," Ethan agreed, knowing full well the lecture he'd get from Grady relating to his actions later. *Should've taken me up on lunch then when I asked*, he thought, a little spitefully.

He was sure there wasn't any risk. He was a sandman, after all, and Marcus was one vampire. *A Class Five against a Class Three*, he mused. He could take care of himself easily.

"Splendid. Come with me to Dacey's place." Marcus smiled. "I think I might be able to help you with your problem if you can help me with one of mine."

"Really?" Ethan was instantly hopeful. He glanced across the street to where Grady's car was parallel parked. "Do you want a ride?"

"I'd prefer to walk," Marcus replied. "The sunlight is still a comforting new development for me. It makes me...optimistic."

"Then we'll walk together," Ethan smiled. "I can come back for the car later. It's not far."

"You're a true gentleman, Ethan Roam," Marcus complimented as they picked up stride together down the sidewalk. "I can definitely see the appeal."

Ethan blushed and grinned into his coffee cup's lid as he took a confident sip.

Twelve: All Good Things

EDWIN QUINN ROLLED up the *Shady Pines Gazette* with disgust, after only reviewing the first few headlines, and slapped the paper on the diner's table, opting to use the periodical as a coaster for his Guinness instead.

"The world is a terrible place full of horrible people," he stated as a waitress shuffled by and quickly picked up their empty dishes. He and Grady had finished an only mildly awkward reunion lunch at a small steakhouse and were now enjoying a couple of drinks to shake the edge off.

"Mmm, yes," Grady concurred, finishing a sip of his own and setting the glass down carefully with his good hand. He'd imbibed another elixir that morning to manage his pain, but the added alcohol was definitely doing its part to numb things as well.

"I try not to pay attention to the news," he continued. "It never tells me anything I want to hear."

"Too true." Edwin nodded. He leaned forward on his elbows and rested his chin on the back of his hands, which were connected through interlocking fingers, and quietly asked, "So, how did things go last night?"

Grady held up his makeshift cast, "Is this not enough indication?"

"Enough to inspire my inquiry. I've been eying the monstrosity for the past half hour. That wrap looks terribly unprofessional," Edwin smirked.

"I did notice. And, I think we're making progress on the issue," Grady responded optimistically regarding the vampires. "Although, my injury certainly slows that progress down. I won't be able to do any field work for a while. I'll have to leave that up to the others."

"What a strange life you lead," Edwin mused. Grady sensed a pleasant air of fascination in his voice. He was relieved to know if his father was going to be around, then at least he was accepting.

"Yes, far from hills and horses." Grady smiled, reminiscing. "It's very odd to think, had things gone as planned, I would now be following in your footsteps. Most likely married and I'd probably have children of my own who would be dashing around, complaining about having to muck stalls when they had made weekend plans."

"You hated mucking stalls." Edwin gave a hearty laugh. "If there was a chore I could give you to ruin your day, that was the one."

"Does anyone like mucking stalls? If so, I hope I never meet him," Grady said with amusement. His smile slowly faded, though, as those familiar memories of the past, which haunted him, ghosted through his mind to remind him why things had not ended up as such after all.

Edwin curved the conversation. "Do you still plan on it? Marrying, I mean."

Surprised, Grady's focus snapped keenly to his father. It certainly wasn't a question he'd expected to be asked. It wasn't one he'd even asked himself.

He grew quiet with introspection as he considered the idea and his fingertips lightly fumbled with the edges of his napkin. He glanced over his father's shoulder and his eyes rested on a yellow neon sign hanging on the distressed shiplap wall amidst numerous framed vintage travel photos. The sign read, *All Good Things Are Wild and Free.*

If he hadn't already been thinking of Ethan, then this would have surely caused him to do so. A surreal fact, as incongruous as that sounded, he was wholeheartedly and helplessly bound by love to a radiant creature, not entirely of his own realm. Who, in the whole of existence, had the ability at any given moment to be more "wild and free" than Ethan Roam? And who was he—a mere mortal man, barely holding the threads of his own meager fabricated life together—to ever stop him from fulfilling that potential? Love was enough to bring him back this time. Marriage might prevent him from ever leaving. Grady hadn't enough selfishness in his heart to demand such a thing from someone he felt he wasn't even entirely sure he deserved.

But what if he did ask? The idea became an immediate and intense temptation he felt root inside him. He silently cursed his father, for now he was plagued with a desire for something he was certain he would never obtain.

"As you said," he answered with guarded trepidation. "I lead a strange life. Hardly makes sense to plan a future when I have no idea what today will bring."

"Ah, but you see, *that* is the truth of life. For everyone. So perhaps yours isn't so strange after all." Edwin shrugged and took another sip of his stout.

Grady had to tip his hat to the man. He was still excellent at putting him in his place. Perhaps, he was right. He lived every day like he may not have a future. Maybe he should start living them as though he would.

"What a terrifying thought," Grady said out loud, in spite of himself.

"What is?" Edwin raised a brow and set his empty drink down.

"What?" Grady hadn't realized his slip until it was too late. He shook the idea off. "Nothing...I was thinking of work."

Edwin smirked, not falling for the lie. "Where is your...Ethan? I haven't had much of a chance to get to know him yet."

"I'm not sure where he is at the moment, but I know where I am. In the dog house," Grady revealed, self-chastising. "I cocked things up earlier and inadvertently brushed him off to spend time with you. I know he's ticked off because he was incredibly understanding about the whole thing. He wears the moral high ground well."

"Oh, my. Don't go getting into domestic rows on my account," Edwin advised. "We could have rescheduled."

"It's fine." Grady waved his concern off. "He'll recover. I'm only annoyed at myself for being short-sighted, but when is that new?"

"As I've learned with your mother: give them time and then give them flowers." Edwin offered his expertise with a lighthearted wink.

"You know, I might take your advice on that." Grady smiled and finished off his drink. "These days, it seems I'm constantly in a position where I need all the help I can get."

"As long as you're willing to take it then everything should turn out fine," Edwin advised.

Grady pulled out his card to pay the waitress when she came by to check on them.

"Would you like to come to the office tonight?" Grady offered. "Ethan should be there. You can get a little more of an idea of what exactly we do."

"You're only offering because you need a ride," Edwin jested. He'd had to drive them to lunch since Grady was injured, and Ethan had taken his vehicle without asking, certainly out of spite.

Grady laughed. "Really, though. You're welcome to join me."

"It would be my pleasure." Edwin grinned. The two rose from their table to leave. "We should stop by a florist on the way."

"The markup on roses will be horrendous this time of year," Grady pointed out practically as they left.

"Don't be cheap, son. Another thing your mother taught me." Edwin patted him on the back.

Thirteen: Wild & Free

THEY'D ENDED UP on the bedroom floor by early evening. Casually sprawled out between carefully sorted piles of Dacey's belongings. Ethan leaned back on a few crimson throw pillows, propped up against the side of the bed, with one leg outstretched and the other bent to steady a scrapbook he was currently engrossed in.

Marcus lay informally on his side next to him, his head resting on his fist as he used his elbow to hold himself up. Ethan was hungrily devouring the words on the pages before him. Dacey Sinnett had quite a compelling past.

They were letters. Old, handwritten confessions from Dacey himself. Some were addressed to a friend and others appeared to be written simply for his own benefit with no particular addressee. They conveyed a vivid summary of the life he led before Ethan, or even Grady, knew him. Parts of the letters had been smudged or burned and were now illegible. Some were even ripped and only contained half of a story. Confessions they were, though. His deepest thoughts and darkest moments. Ethan was fascinated.

Marcus had spent the day rehashing his past with Dacey to Ethan. At least, he shared enough to strike a chord with Ethan. In return, Ethan opened up about his own relationship and also told Marcus of the brief time he'd known Dacey. They both seemed surprised by how easily they confided in one another.

Now Marcus was letting Ethan read a few letters which he was certain would validate his claims and motivate him to join his cause.

"So, what happened? What went wrong?" Ethan asked, looking over at Marcus and closing the album as he finished. "I mean, he writes of adamantly wanting to defeat this demonic guy who was holding you two apart, but then the letters abruptly stop. Obviously, you two won. So, why weren't you together in the end?"

Marcus offered a sullen gaze and took a purposefully deep breath which sounded heavy with regret. "I'm afraid in the end I pushed him too hard. I expected too much. You see, I wanted him all to myself, but you know how Dacey was...with everyone. Sometimes there are hearts you can't tame no matter how much you sacrifice. I suppose that's why he was drawn to Grady. The hunter preferred him as a wild animal. They were both out for blood in their own ways."

Ethan was almost sorry he'd even asked. Unfortunately, early in his training with Grady, he'd been made privy to the fact Grady and Dacey's dalliance was purely primal. That part of Grady's past wasn't something he was particularly fond of being reminded about, but he usually did a pretty good job of not letting it get to him. In the moment, however, he experienced a deep pang of jealousy and disgust. His relationship with Grady wasn't like that at all. It was based on comradery, respect, and love, which was mostly good but partly frustrating. There were definitely times when Ethan fantasized of purely carnal connections and knowing Grady had participated in one with someone else made him envious beyond rational thought. Especially since all Grady ever seemed to do was focus on protecting Ethan, trying to keep him "safe" when he'd apparently let Dacey be as reckless and free-spirited as he wished.

Although, he recognized that hadn't turned out the best for him in the end. He felt guilty for his selfish emotions. He'd watched Grady stand by and let Dacey sacrifice himself to save Ethan. Why? Because of the stark truth. Grady loved Ethan, not Dacey.

Seeing the gloom in Marcus's eyes now, he was thankful at least that relationship was part of his lover's past because, for the vampire, things were the other way around. He'd lost the man he loved to the desire for hollow pleasure instead. A pain Ethan surely never wanted to endure.

"I don't even know what to say," Ethan replied apologetically.

"Better to have loved and lost, or so they say," Marcus said as he moved to sit upright. He shrugged as he leaned in toward Ethan. "I'm not angry. I could never really be angry with Dacey. I simply wish I could have convinced him to give me a fair chance to please him eternally. I loved him with more passion and devotion than the culmination of all of his admirers. I still do. And I always will."

"I liked Dacey and everything," Ethan said. "But I honestly don't understand him. I mean, if I were in his shoes, I'd never let you go. You're handsome, smart, intriguing... You look like one of those guys from the cover of a romance novel. Anyone would be lucky to have you, and I know that's cliché as hell, but it's true."

He gave the blond vampire a warm smile, surprised at his own boldness to pay him such high compliments.

Marcus looked delighted. He let out a small bashful laugh and ran his fingers through his own curly hair. He leaned his head back on the side of the bed, biting his bottom lip with a hint of unprecedented shyness.

"Thank you, Ethan. That's the kindest thing anyone has ever said to me in the whole of my existence." He shifted his gaze to him and grinned. Ethan believed he was sincerely appreciative.

"You must not have known very many nice people then," Ethan remarked.

"No. I can't honestly say I have," Marcus sighed with resigned acceptance. He looked at Ethan's hand, which rested on the floor next to him and boldly took it in his. He squeezed his palm with genuine gratitude.

Ethan felt his face grow hot, worried he'd crossed an invisible line of decency considering the dichotomy that he was talking to the ex-boyfriend of his current boyfriend's last unofficial boyfriend.

Man, relationships are confusing, he thought and then quickly scoured his mind for any valid topic to keep the conversation from getting awkward as he released his hand from the vampire's.

"So, you said you might be able to help me find a way to travel with Grady if I can help you with your problem," Ethan reminded him. He wiped his palms, which had become nervously sweaty, on his jeans. "Are you ready to share what exactly that problem is?"

"I've been building up to that," Marcus explained. "I didn't tell you of my love life because I'm some hopeless, angsty, brooding lover. I mean, clearly I am, but that wasn't my sole motivation in revealing the past to you. I needn't an audience to perform romantic soliloquies. You see, my problem *is* your problem. Rather, we both want the same thing."

"We do?" Ethan shifted into a more upright position from the floor, extremely curious to find out where he was headed.

"I want you to be able to travel with others in tow as well. In fact, I need you to be. Because I want to you fetch someone for me," Marcus revealed. "I want you to bring Dacey back."

Ethan's heart dropped. Even if he knew how to travel with a companion, there was no way for him to know where Dacey was, or if he was even still alive.

"Marcus, I—" Ethan was going to explain his reservations, but Marcus promptly hopped to his feet and held a hand out to him. Ethan accepted the gesture and rose to meet him, nearly nose to nose. Marcus lingered there a moment longer than was necessary, letting Ethan's breath fall against him. Slowly, he released Ethan's hand.

"I already know what you're going to say," Marcus persisted. "But I have everything worked out. I can help you learn to travel with others, and I know how we can find Dacey. I only need you to trust me."

Ethan hardly believed what he was hearing. Marcus would help him achieve the one thing he wanted more than anything else and all he had to do was be his friend?

"Of course," Ethan agreed, his heart pounding eagerly. "I trust you. One hundred percent."

Marcus smiled victoriously and grabbed Ethan by the back of his neck, pulling him closer until their foreheads rested lightly against each other's. Marcus closed his eyes in what appeared to be joyful relief.

Ethan's heartbeat was now so pronounced he was sure the vampire could hear. For a moment, he thought Marcus might try to kiss him, but instead, he simply whispered.

"Thank you. That's all I needed to hear." He then pulled back and motioned for Ethan to follow him. Marcus led him out of the room, down the dark hallway of the small house, and to a locked basement door.

Ethan hesitated. His last experience in a basement hadn't exactly gone well and there was no reason whatsoever he should trust Marcus, even though he said he did out of desperate optimism. In fact, Grady had explicitly instructed him to stay away from the vampire.

His loyalty and intuition struggled to hold him back but his curiosity and determination to master his talents were blindingly persuasive.

Marcus had already reached the bottom of the small basement staircase and flipped on a light switch. "Are you coming or not? I promise I'm not going to lock you down here. There aren't any captives or dead bodies if that's what you're thinking. You said you trusted me."

"Yeah, of course I'm coming." Ethan pushed his doubts and anxiety back into the inner-Pandora's box of emotion from which they'd begun to escape and made his way down, consciously and cautiously, leaving the door open.

Once inside, he was surprised to see the room was actually very well kept. Dacey had converted the space into a small studio apartment, complete with a bed, a television, and a bathroom; pretty much everything one would need, except for a kitchen—which, of course, a vampire wouldn't need.

Marcus had purposefully made his way to an antique steamer trunk that sat at the end of an ornate, black, wooden, queen-sized four-poster bed. He knelt before the ebony chest and produced a key from his pocket, which he used to unlock its golden latch.

Ethan caught sight of a camera behind him, attached to a tripod, facing the bed. A small glass table sat beside with various accessories and devices clearly intended for specific pleasurable use. He began to question his decision to follow the vampire.

"Um, why are we here?" His voice produced a slight, abashed tremble. He shoved his hands into his pockets, feeling insecure. His fingers touched the stranger's phone again, which he'd forgotten in the course of the day's events. Grady had advised him to destroy the phone, but Chris had prevented it from being traced, and at the moment, it was the only lead they had on the gang of vampires. He still wanted to search her contact list and messages for clues. The vampires seemed to think she possessed valuable information, even if she denied as much.

Marcus stopped, quixotic, following Ethan's gaze to the camera, toys, and bondage gear nearby.

"We're not here for that." Marcus smirked with mild amusement. "Unless, of course, you want to be."

Ethan nearly fainted.

"Joking," Marcus reassured. He unfastened the last two latches on the trunk. "That's Dacey for you. Leaving everything out in the open. I wouldn't recommend snooping around here if you don't want an unpleasant surprise. Especially not if you notice any photos lying around. You might see some things that would break your heart... I know I did."

Ethan didn't have to think twice to understand the implication of the statement. His mood plummeted and his throat instantly hardened with jealousy. A few sparks of energy tingled his fingertips. Crossing his arms, he slipped his hands under his armpits as he attempted to maintain control.

"Again, I ask, why are we here?" He repeated, clenching his jaw. He felt the psi pulse building up inside him, and he knew he had to practice self-restraint.

"For this," Marcus answered simply, producing an old tome from the trunk. The book was such an oddity of age, it swiftly distracted Ethan from being upset. The leather binding looked practically ancient.

"Another scrapbook?" He guessed lamely. He had a pretty good feeling the antique wasn't any such thing.

"Before I tell you what this is, I need you to show me something," Marcus began when he was interrupted by a ringtone.

Ethan fumbled to pull out his own phone. He saw the time and realized he should be at the office by now.

"It's Grady. I'm running late. I have to take this," he said. But he hesitated. He wasn't sure what he'd say. He knew Grady wouldn't be very understanding of the situation.

Marcus simply gestured to the instrument by the wall behind Ethan. "Fine, but would you mind grabbing that handkerchief off the piano? There's a lot of dust on this old book."

"Sure." Ethan nodded, thinking nothing of the request. He strolled over to the small piano Dacey kept stored there. He was about to answer the call, as he reached for the blue pocket square of fabric, when a stack of photos sitting next to the handkerchief caught his eye.

He saw the images immediately and a brief second later he finally registered what he was seeing. Several nude photos, fanned out, as though on display. All of them of Grady.

His face wasn't shown in them, but Ethan knew who he was looking at. There was no mistake. His naked form was unforgettable and every inch was ingrained in Ethan's memory. Every muscle, every curve, and every scar.

But there was another body in the photos as well. Someone else was touching him. Someone else's lips were pressed against his skin. Someone else was bringing him to ecstasy. And that someone was Dacey.

He might as well be suffocating in his own nightmare as despair washed over him. He looked to Marcus in disbelief only to see the vampire wore a smug smile of triumph.

"Never mind," Marcus remarked, with a cold air of indifference. "On second thought, I think the dirt adds character."

Ethan's entire body went rigid with fury.

His phone rang continuously the entire time he was getting a firsthand look at his lover's past. He angrily smashed 'decline' on the screen and then turned his phone off completely.

"Why?" He asked, rage bubbling up inside. "Why would you do this to me? You set me up. You knew I would see them!"

Marcus was now standing, clutching the old book to his chest.

Ethan couldn't control himself, and Marcus became the target of his wrath. His body tingled with the electric sensation of consuming energy, and he released a pulse of wild white psychic funneled light in Marcus's direction. Under ordinary circumstances, the blast would have incinerated a vampire as the magic was essentially a burning mass of starfire, but Marcus was a daywalker now and still very much supernatural. Instead, the pulse hit him with extreme force, scorching his clothes, and knocking him off his feet. His body was thrust backward into the table of risqué objects—some undeniably used in the photos—which went flying, glass table shattering, as they unceremoniously scattered across the room.

Ethan instantly regretted his actions. He was infuriated at him for such a sadistic trick, but he also knew Marcus had most likely felt the same helpless grief he had when he'd first found the photos.

He didn't have to feel bad for long, though. Marcus was laughing. The reaction was unnervingly out of place.

"Because you deserved to know the truth. You needed to," Marcus answered as he pulled himself back to his feet. He locked eyes with Ethan in a silent bid for dominance.

"I already knew the truth!" Ethan shouted. "I didn't need to *see* it!"

"No, you definitely did." Marcus remained terrifyingly upbeat and gazed at the tome in his hands. An eerie smirk of victory played on his lips as he turned to face the book's cover toward Ethan.

Ethan saw an imprint of a seven-pointed star and various inscriptions glowing a vibrant translucent blue. They shimmered, radiating with the same stardust light he'd just produced.

"You see, that's what you were missing." Marcus beamed at him. "Fire. True selfish rage. I had suspected it and now I see I was right. This was a theory I developed when Dacey and I were trapped with Findlay McCrea, the demon from the letters. He preyed on feelings and manipulated people with them. Emotions are as varying and uniquely precise as color. A full spectrum, if you will. Certain creatures, like Findlay—and yourself—wield their powers through them. You have to experience them all in order to conquer them all. However, you hadn't yet felt the searing torture of envy. Now you have. And now we can begin your training."

"But sandmen are supposed to be emotionless," Ethan disputed, recalling what Chris had told him the night before, disregarding the fact he already knew he was different than the sandmen who had come before him.

"No one is emotionless. Your information is flawed. Or at least skewed," Marcus corrected. "I said *conquer* them, did I not? Sandmen have to ascend to a higher form of enlightenment. You have to control your emotions so you can command them, instead of letting them command you. That's why your ancestors appeared emotionless. They were perfectly balanced creatures of zen. You could have destroyed me if you'd kept going. But you stopped yourself. He commanded your power."

"What is that?" Ethan asked warily as he eyed the astrological-looking book.

"A codex." Marcus held the tome out to him.

Ethan swore the inscriptions on the front looked familiar. Something he'd read before, a long time ago. In fact, he was pretty sure he was reading them now. The characters were foreign, alien-looking even, but they translated themselves into Latin in his mind as he read them. Apprehensive, he didn't dare touch the book. He left the artifact in Marcus's possession.

"*Somnium Iter In Maledictionem?*" He spoke the words out loud, even though he was certain he didn't understand much Latin. Strangely, it now appeared he was fluent in the language.

"Is that what it says?" Marcus glanced at the cover with surprised fascination. Obviously, he'd never known precisely what the codex was, but the expression that registered on his face indicated a lot of things now made much more sense than they had previously.

"The Dream Traveler's Curse," Ethan verified. He studied Marcus with renewed interest. "Where did you get this? And how do you know so much about sandmen? You invited me here because of more than my frail connection to Dacey, didn't you?"

Marcus approached him slowly. "Frail wouldn't be the word I would use... I asked you to trust me. Do you?"

Ethan didn't answer. He wasn't sure he trusted anything anymore.

Marcus reached past him and scooped up the incriminating photos. He looked at them momentarily and frowned, sorrow cast over his expression. He shoved one into Ethan's hoodie pocket and put the rest into his own back pocket.

"We said we were similar to each other's lovers, but the truth is we're not much different, you and I," Marcus said, studying Ethan. "In fact, I think you'll find I can be your greatest ally and your best friend if you'll give me half a chance."

Ethan's compassion and growing inquisitiveness broke down his cautious barriers. He may not have appreciated Marcus's methods but, in the end, the vampire had made good on his word. He'd willingly given him valuable information and offered him an actual artifact of his ancestry. Not only that, but he seemed to sincerely have the knowledge and resources to help Ethan achieve his full potential.

And he was right, Ethan acquiesced as he considered the photo that now plagued his pocket. They shared a mutual pain. There were definitely solid building blocks to build a friendship on.

"All right." Ethan nodded, taking a deep decisive breath. "Where do we start?"

"From the beginning, of course," Marcus instructed with a sly smile, handing over the codex. "Now, open the book and remove your clothes."

Fourteen: Magic & Malice

"HE'S NOT ANSWERING his phone, and now the damned thing is going directly to voicemail." Grady sighed as he worriedly paced the front lobby of his office.

"Cue the super spy. That's what I'm here for," Chris reassured, and with a few quick hand motions, he pulled up their surveillance screens and digital maps.

"Weird." He frowned, scratching the side of his head as he synced with the tracing system he'd established in the Jaguar. "According to this, he's been parked at the cafe since this morning. Must be writing one hell of a novel."

"Ethan hated having to write essays for school. I doubt he'd ever sit long enough to write a novel," Karen chimed in with her own concern.

She and Benny both surveyed the monitors over Chris's shoulder. Edwin stood back, appraising the setup with awe, since practical magic was still a relatively new experience for him.

"You don't think he was kidnapped, do you? Should I go try to sniff out a trail?" Benny practically whimpered. Karen looked to Grady with dismay.

"Well, I'm sure as hell not going to stand around here waiting to find out," Grady stated firmly. "Dammit, I wish I had a tracking device implanted in *him,* but I know he'd never allow it."

"Whoa there, Hunter," Chris advised calmly. "I'm starting to see why the Order wanted to recruit you."

"*I'd* never allow it. Is that him?" Karen pointed to something flashing on the right-hand screen. Everyone moved in closer to take a look. Sure enough, an energy flux had gone off a few blocks away from the cafe. The activity was precisely the type of occurrence they'd seen with Ethan.

"I thought we told him not to use his powers," Chris said gruffly, slamming his palm on the desk in frustration.

"Unless he's in a situation where he doesn't have a choice," Grady quickly defended. "Zoom in on the coordinates."

Chris aligned his fingers to form a rectangle, using his magic as he pulled them back again to focus in on the exact location. "He's funneling a pretty large amount of energy," he observed.

"That's Dacey's house!" Benny spoke up, a low growl sounding afterward.

"Dammit! I knew better than to tempt him, but I didn't listen to myself." Grady pulled his own hair in frustration.

Karen leaned toward him, seeking answers. "What do you mean? What's happened?"

Grady wheeled around and faced Edwin. "The keys to your rental car. I need them!"

Edwin swiftly handed them over. Grady threw them into Chris's hands and motioned for him to follow.

"We have to leave *now*! He's in danger," Grady instructed as he ran out the front door of the lobby. Chris followed with urgency.

"YES! YES!" MARCUS exclaimed passionately. "Ethan, you're amazing!"

Ethan stood nude in a transmutation circle Marcus had scrawled onto the floor with a stick of charcoal. He'd been impressed by the vampire's self-restraint when he sliced his palm and let his blood drip onto the drawing. The magic circle pulsed with energy. The vampire made no move to try to drink from him. He simply stood by his side, waiting patiently.

Ethan was shimmering, his skin glowing and twinkling as though he were a walking nebula. He focused his thoughts and energy on one goal: opening a portal in the basement that would lead them directly to the Dream World. The codex had explicitly defined instructions.

Marcus had volunteered to be his guinea pig, motivated by the prospect of finding Dacey. The vampire was holding the codex up so Ethan could refer to the pages when needed. He was very nearly successful as reality began to warp in front of them and the veil between dimensions began to rip open.

He'd opened portals to other dimensions before but never one that was a direct line to the universal subconscious. At least not intentionally. Now, however, was the time to practice fulfillment of intent.

A riotous blast of gunfire and footsteps from upstairs broke Ethan's concentration. The small portal that had begun to take shape quickly disappeared and his energy flow fluxed back inside. His body returned to its full human form. The transmutation circle, once vibrant and glowing from his influence, now reverted back to nothing but a plain, dormant scrawl on the floor.

"Ethan!" A stern, frantic voice called out from upstairs.

"Oh, for fuck's sake!" Marcus looked as though he wanted to throw the codex across the room in anger but thankfully did not. Instead, he hurried to hide the book in the trunk from which it was produced. "Don't tell him anything! He'll never allow this!"

Ethan scrambled to grab his clothes but wasn't able to put them on fast enough. Marcus was much quicker in his reaction and had already covered the transmutation circle with the comforter from the bed. All Ethan managed to do was get his boxers on by the time Grady and Chris came trampling down the staircase and halted as they reached the bottom. They stared at him, still semi-nude, kneeling in front of a very smug—looking vampire.

Chris nudged Grady lightly from behind. "Something tells me he wasn't in danger..."

"He's going to be. Ethan!" Grady practically spat. "Would you care to explain?"

"Uh..." Ethan blushed fiercely, clutching the ball of clothing against his torso. He should have thought this through. His mind was completely blank on excuses. He didn't know how to tell Grady the truth, but he hated for him to think the worst.

"He shouldn't have to explain anything," Marcus defended, rising to his feet and planting his hands on his hips with condescending indignation. He curled his upper lip snidely, sticking his nose in the air and treating them as unwelcome guests. "Isn't breaking and entering still illegal? I should call the police at once."

"Oh, shut up, Marcus! This isn't even your house," Grady snapped.

"As much as it pains me to say, perhaps you should put on your trousers, Ethan," Marcus advised evenly.

"Yes, probably a good place to start." Grady glared at Ethan.

Ethan, completely mortified, clumsily re-dressed as he tried desperately to think of something to say that would magically rectify the situation. Turns out magic is useful for most everything but an awkward situation.

"Wow. I have to admit, this was really not what I expected us to walk in on," Chris scoffed, trying to break the tension. "Like, at all. Are those dildos on the floor? Why is the furniture broken? What kind of kinky—"

"Shut up, Chris!" Grady demanded through clenched teeth.

"Sure thing, boss." Chris motioned zipping his lips and sat on the bottom step of the staircase, still surveying the mess around the room. He leaned back, a curious spectator.

"The only person I want to hear anything from right now is Ethan," Grady advised the other two sternly. His gaze was steadily held on Ethan who wanted nothing more than to escape it.

"This isn't what it looks like" was all Ethan thought to say.

"I've heard that line before," Chris remarked. Grady reached back with his free hand and shoved Chris to quiet him.

"Really," Grady pressed, reluctant to accept his weak defense. "Because the state of this room is painting a pretty vivid picture."

Marcus smirked mischievously.

"I promise." Ethan's voice shook. He looked to Grady in earnest, hoping he would believe him.

Despite the distrust chiseled on Grady's face, he acquiesced. "All right. I want you to tell me the truth. Later. Away from here. Away from *him*." He shot a hateful look at Marcus.

Ethan nodded solemnly, grateful Grady seemed willing to grant him the benefit of the doubt. Grady motioned for him to leave with Chris.

"C'mon, kid. We have to think up some decent excuse to tell your mom. She thought this was a rescue mission, not an amateur skin-flick audition," Chris said, slapping a hand on Ethan's shoulder as they ascended the stairs and left. Grady hung behind.

Once they were out of earshot, Grady rounded on Marcus with a murderous glare.

"What were you doing with my sandman?" he demanded. He kept his tone low but still brimming with venom.

The blond vampire nonchalantly pulled some photographs from his pocket and slapped them to Grady's chest. Confused, Grady took the opportunity to look at the risqué photos, and his guts immediately twisted in panic.

"Don't worry. He didn't do anything you wouldn't do," Marcus remarked coldly. He took a seat on the trunk by the bed, crossing his legs and arms defiantly.

Any anger Grady may have had with Ethan immediately dissipated and reformed further fueling his hatred toward Marcus. He shuffled through the pictures helplessly, regretting his past actions depicted in the haunting images. He paused on one that showed his body pressed against Dacey's as the raven-haired vampire was bound and gagged on the bed.

Ethan had seen these. There was no better explanation for his actions.

Perhaps he was getting even; attempting to kill the pain with what he thought would be a justified betrayal. Grady certainly hoped he was smarter, and more importantly, kinder than that. But who was he to blame

Ethan even if he wasn't? Any one of those photos was enough to rip a man's heart in two, and there were several.

Grady knew visiting Marcus might have been a mistake, but he'd had no idea how quickly and how effectively the evil vampire could work his angle. He hated to imagine what might have happened tonight had he waited a little while longer to seek out Ethan.

"Is that really what this is about?" Grady grilled him, his voice choking up a bit. He was filled with misery, self-torment, and a healthy dose of remorse. "Revenge over Dacey?"

He reached for a stake in his jacket, ready to defend himself against the vampire, should he decide to strike. A rather large part of his psyche wanted to slay Marcus right then and be done with him. The vampire could never hurt Ethan, never touch him, if he didn't exist, and Grady could put that part of his past fully behind him.

Marcus must have expected his thoughts. "As much as the fact pains you, hunter, you can't kill me. Ethan would never forgive you. We're intimate friends now, you see."

"Is that right?" Grady scoffed. Marcus simply smiled back with loathing of equal measure.

"He said he'd tell you the truth," Marcus advised. "Why don't you ask him? Anyway, he'd be much safer in my company than he'd ever be in yours. As it is, he appears in constant peril. We all know what your influence did to the last man you touched. At least, I know how to keep my lovers alive, so long as they're with me."

"Stay away from him! This is your last and only warning!" Grady tore the pictures and threw them at Marcus; they fluttered to the floor, pieces of a sordid puzzle. He decided to leave the stake where it was, for another day. As much as he hated the wretched bloodsucker, he was right. Ethan would never forgive him if he killed Marcus. Not when he appeared to be so deeply caught up in his manipulation.

"I'm not the one you have to worry about." Marcus smirked coyly, standing again with renewed self-righteous conviction. "Your boy will be back of his own accord. He won't be able to stay away. He'll need me. *Want* me."

"Have you done something to him? Cast some spell?" Grady clenched the fist of his good hand, barely holding back his desire to eradicate the contemptuous vampire before him.

"Don't be ridiculous. We're very much alike, that's all. Our stars are aligned, one might say." Marcus remained too calm. He gestured at Grady's injured hand. "You know, you should probably see a real doctor for that, *human*."

"He *won't* be back. And you *will* stay away," Grady warned again with finality before turning to leave. He'd gone halfway up the stairs before Marcus responded.

"You're wrong, Hunter!" The vampire called out as Grady decidedly ignored him and kept walking. "He won't be able to stay away from me! He'll come back to me because of his *desire* to. Our threads are intertwined. You wait and see!"

Grady slammed the door shut as he left.

Fifteen: Transmutation

"GRADY, I'M SO sorry. I swear it was nothing—" Ethan began to ramble a mortified apology as soon as Grady strolled up to the car where he and Chris had been waiting.

"Get in," Grady interrupted. He rounded to the other side without so much as a glance at Ethan and got into the back seat of the driver's side.

At least he's still willing to sit next to me, Ethan gloomily consoled himself as he got in.

"Wasn't aware the job description included 'chauffeur' when I signed up, but sure, why not? As long as I don't have to play relationship counselor too," Chris muttered jokingly as he got behind the wheel and quickly drove them the hell away from the vampire's house.

The awkward silence was palpable with tension.

"I'm gonna give us some cruising music if that's all right," Chris commented. He cast a spell on the car radio to tune to a signal he must have known by heart. A low blend of dark electronic music began to play. Ethan had never heard the melody before, but based on the few lyrics he heard, he was fairly certain the song was French.

He then noticed a beautifully wrapped bouquet of roses laying on the seat beside him. He had his arms crossed, as did Grady for that matter, but he curiously looked to his partner, in spite of his introverted posture.

"What are those for?" he asked warily, hoping not to get the cold shoulder. If he could only break the ice somehow and explain everything, then he knew their relationship would be fine.

"Well, they *were* for you," Grady answered, still refusing to look in his direction. "I was feeling guilty for not spending the day with you. But now I think I'll give them to Chris as a consolation for wasting his time."

Grady grabbed the flowers and chucked them into the front passenger seat, almost a bit too forcefully.

"Aww, shucks," Chris said, with a playful Western drawl. "I feel so appreciated."

"Would you please turn off that god-awful music?" Grady requested. He rubbed his temples in dire vexation. "It's giving me a headache."

"But it's Witch House! The songs of my people," Chris protested in jest. In the rearview mirror, he added a dramatic pout for effect, but he turned the volume down enough to placate Grady.

"You have to let me explain." Ethan couldn't stand the misconception being drawn out any longer.

"You had plenty of opportunity to explain when I was calling you repeatedly earlier, but you didn't answer your phone," Grady pointed out. "Of course, now I know why—"

"Stop!" Ethan interrupted, now frustrated. "Just stop, okay? I wasn't doing anything wrong. I'm sorry I didn't answer your calls, but I was..."

He paused, trying to find a way of explaining the situation without giving away knowledge of the codex. This issue wasn't that he didn't trust Grady; it was that he didn't trust Grady to trust him.

Grady looked at him expectantly.

Ethan took a deep, calming breath and tried to give the most concise and simplistic account of events he could. Despite Marcus's pleas for total secrecy, Ethan couldn't lie to Grady. Not completely, anyway.

"I ran into Marcus totally by chance today. We ended up talking for a long time. Mostly concerning Dacey...and you. But then he told me he could help me with my traveling problems. Opening portals and transporting people safely with me at will. That's what we were doing—trying to make my powers more effective. He offered himself as a test subject. I swear, that's all. And I'm sorry if he made the situation seem any different. He just really doesn't like you," he revealed.

"Despite the scantily clad state I found you in, you can still be so innocent," Grady replied. He sounded defeated. "The fact you'd ever believe Marcus would cross your path 'by chance' is proof enough."

"I'm going to swing you kids by your car at the cafe," Chris stated as he drove, knowing full well they weren't paying him any attention.

"And why exactly did this experiment require you to be nude?" Grady grilled Ethan, playing his last doubt card.

"We were doing a spell," Ethan justified, though he himself didn't sound quite convinced his nudity was necessary. "He said all rituals are more effective if you remove modern effects like clothing and personal belongings."

"I'm sure he did. Vampires..." Grady smirked now and chuckled slightly. Ethan hoped that was a good sign. After a moment, things clicked and Ethan realized Grady might be right. He'd been played by a lecherous vampire; at least in part.

"Well, anyway, the whole thing was just spell work. I promise," Ethan finished, feeling stupid.

"I believe you," Grady consoled. He took Ethan's hand in his to prove so. Appreciative, Ethan smiled.

"Did the spell work?" Grady wondered.

Ethan shrugged. "Not sure. We were interrupted." He glanced at him pointedly, but he wasn't upset.

"How did you run into Marcus precisely?" True to form, Grady was already back to the business of puzzling out mysteries.

"Yes, and might I interject we specifically requested you *not* use your powers," Chris added over his shoulder. "Here's a pro-tip: Vampires are only ever interested in helping themselves. Besides, whatever problem you're having can't be solved through traditional magic. Other than the abilities you're able to hone naturally by yourself, there aren't going to be any outside forces that can make you more powerful. Unless, maybe you had one of the Sandman Artifacts, but that's impossible. They were lost hundreds of years ago. Also, the Transmutation of Azoth would do the trick, but that is precisely the thing we want to avoid."

"He's a daywalker now. Blame Vivian," Ethan quickly answered Grady before giving Chris his rapt attention. He'd said a number of fascinating things. "Sandman Artifacts? Like what? Why hadn't you said something about them before?"

"Uh, because they don't exist anymore and are therefore irrelevant," Chris answered in a matter-of-fact manner.

"You have to tell me everything you know!" Ethan insisted, practically pushing his entire body up against the back of the passenger seat to get closer to Chris, as though that would somehow get him closer to the truth.

"Ethan, is there something you're not telling us about this spell you were doing?" Grady narrowed his eyes.

Before Ethan could decide to come clean, a ringing sounded in his pocket. Startled, he pulled the phone out to see who was calling.

"Oh, sure. You'll answer phone calls when they're not mine." Grady rolled his eyes and gestured with his good hand as if to add, *of course.*

"It's not my phone." Ethan's voice was hollow as he stared at the glowing screen of the woman's phone in shock.

"What?" Grady leaned in his direction. The phone kept ringing, but Ethan didn't answer. Instead, he held the screen up for Grady to see.

As expected, Grady looked just as surprised as he was.

The phone repeated the ring once more and continued to flash the name onscreen.

Incoming Call: DACEY

The caller disconnected as a loud gunshot fired through the rear window of their car, fracturing the pane. Startled, Chris swerved and tried to regain control.

Grady and Ethan both ducked for cover and looked around to quickly assess they were all still alive.

"Fuck!" Chris shouted, hitting the gas and pushing the rental car to a highly unsafe speed.

"What's happening?" Ethan panicked.

"You used your powers, kid! Think things through!" Chris reminded him. He swerved erratically through traffic; in an apparent effort to lose whoever was on their tail.

Grady and Ethan were still hunched down, attempting to stay out of the line of fire. They heard a second gunshot, clipping another part of the vehicle.

"Hunters?" Grady asked.

"Sure as demon shit!" Chris confirmed as they fishtailed onto what Ethan guessed was a different road. "And this one is gaining fast! Coming around the left side! Stay down!"

Ethan must have had some inherent need to disobey the most basic orders. He sat up in time to see a dark-helmeted figure on a black, unmarked street bike pull up next to them. The rider was wearing all black bike apparel and matching black leather gloves, but he was also silhouetted in a silvery purplish mist, which Ethan had learned was a telling sign of magic at work.

As he matched their speed, the hunter raised his arm and Ethan saw the handgun. There was no time to think of consequences, only to react.

With adrenaline rushing, Ethan raised his palms and released a pulse of psi energy so powerful everything around them was consumed in a hot, blindingly, bright light. He couldn't see a thing now. He wasn't even sure they were on the road anymore. He swore they were floating.

Sixteen: Death's Warning

"WHY DO THE living never answer their phones?" A familiar, but exasperated, voice lamented from the faceless form cloaked in ebony robes hovering above Ethan. The figure threw its arms in the air, dramatically illustrating its frustration, and then reached out with a black-gloved hand to help Ethan up.

Ethan was lying on his back in a field of vibrant purple and blue flowers of seemingly alien origin. It was twilight, and although not technically dark enough, he saw celestial bodies revolving in the sky at varying rates of speed. He recognized his location at once. He'd somehow ended up in the Dream World.

Disoriented, he reluctantly accepted the help of the mysterious robed individual and found his footing upright. A chill ran through him as he realized he was face-to-face with Death, and he immediately assumed the worst had transpired. Until, of course, the figure pulled its hood off to reveal its true identity.

"Dacey!" Shocked and overjoyed, Ethan threw himself forward, giving Dacey a huge hug.

"I'm so glad you're not dead!" He beamed.

"I'm far past that." Dacey grinned, returning the embrace.

"Wait...are you saying you *are* Death? Is that what the creepy outfit is for? Am I dead?" Ethan released him, stumbling backward.

"Take a deep breath, Ethan. This will go a lot smoother if you don't have a panic attack over every new piece of information handed to you," Dacey advised. "First of all, no. You're not dead. You're unconscious. You managed to create a time flux, which is quite impressive given the fact you're still relatively new to this."

"A time flux?" Ethan repeated, consumed with confusion.

"Essentially, you've pressed pause back home. When you wake up, everything will resume in the moment you left," Dacey explained. "A rather handy power to have in dire straits if you have control. Although, I'm fairly certain you don't. You didn't even know you were capable of such magic, so how could you have possibly intended it?"

"Okay...so that's how I got here. How did *you* get here? I thought you were lost," Ethan pressed, full of suspicion and wonder.

"Well, to answer your first question. Yes, I am Death," Dacey revealed with a slight bow. "Like you, I have the ability to travel realms at will. Unfortunately, unlike you, making contact with mortals on the physical plane isn't in my wheelhouse. Those with special sight—supernaturals—can sense or sometimes even glimpse my presence, but my influence on Earth is strictly confined to the spiritual plane."

Before Ethan even asked, Dacey addressed the obvious forthcoming question, "I didn't survive getting sucked through the dimensional rip you created. On the bright side, neither did your werewolf foe, Marius. And I had help waiting for me on the other side."

"I can't believe this" was all Ethan could manage.

"Well, you'd better because that's the most believable part of any of the things I've come to tell you," Dacey advised with a small sigh, indicating he wasn't happy about the need for their reunion.

He waved his hand to a nearby sinewy tree. The branches appeared to magically grow at a rapid rate toward the ground, wrapping and twisting around one another, until they formed a makeshift bench. Dacey waited for Ethan to join him as he took a seat. Ethan looked to the tree reluctantly but followed suit.

"May I say, I love Grady, but he's doing a terrible job of keeping you protected." Dacey shook his head like an overburdened guardian. "I can't put too much blame on him, though. He is completely human, after all. Sometimes we cosmic entities must step in and handle things ourselves. "

"How did you become Death?" Ethan inquired, trying to remain as open-minded as possible, despite his impending sense of alarm.

"In a way, I always was," Dacey revealed. "You see, humans misinterpret Death. They think it's a creature in and of itself; it's not. Death is a position of power. One I was burdened with eons ago. Others, loyal friends, held the title for me while I was missing, but now I've returned."

"Wait. I... I thought you were a vampire..." Ethan stated.

"I was." Dacey nodded simply. "And before that, I was a man. And before that, I was a handful of other men. And during all of that time, I lost connection with my true self. My real essence resided in every one of them but lay dormant. I was in hiding. I hid within man, through genetics. Similar to you. You've been slightly misinformed, Ethan. The Sandman wasn't your ancestor, not technically. The Sandman has existed within you all along. Within your entire bloodline. He and I were desperate. We didn't want to be found. And for good reason. But I was awakened, and now I've returned to my rightful place to wield my heavy crown and deliver an extremely important message."

"You knew the Sandman? If Death is just a title, then who are you? Really?" Ethan narrowed his eyes, consumed with fascination and fear at the implications.

"I am Mercury," he answered proudly. Gravely, he added, "And I've come to warn you that you will bring humanity to its end."

"Okay, this is clearly a dream." Ethan stood quickly from the makeshift bench of alien flora. He began pacing, concentrating hard to wake himself. His efforts were futile, and he tugged at his hair in frustration, not wanting to believe Dacey's horribly depressing words.

"Not like a traveling dream but like a real one. The kind I used to have before all of this shit started." He instructed himself as though Dacey—or *Mercury*, as he insisted—wasn't there.

"Mortal dreams are never real; that's rather the point," Mercury remarked, patiently. "And you've never been entirely mortal. Every dream you've ever had was a traveling dream, even if you weren't enlightened enough to realize the truth at the time."

Ethan pivoted to face him, crestfallen. He stopped pacing.

"So I'm supposed to simply accept I'm a living apocalypse? Is that what you're telling me?" If this was the unveiling of the final mystery in relation to himself, then he knew it would be far too much to bear. He couldn't fathom shouldering the weight of it all.

Mercury reflected on his poor choice of words. "I suppose it isn't entirely fair to put *all* of the responsibility on your shoulders. This predicament involves me just as much as you. Please sit; you're giving me anxiety, and I already carry enough negative energy inside me as it is."

"Oh, I'm giving *you* anxiety?" Ethan couldn't believe his ostentatious comment. After seeing Mercury would speak no further on the subject until he followed orders, he returned to his seat in submissive resignation.

"Thank you, love," Mercury placated, patting him affectionately on the knee.

"Dacey—Mercury—" Ethan began but was unsure to whom he was speaking.

"You can call me Dacey if you like." The King of the Spirit World decided. "Dacey was my favorite of the lives I've lived, and so I still maintain his features." He grinned, gesturing to his own face. "I retain all of his memories. *My* memories. We've just flipped who is in charge. He's still here, on the inside. We're one and the same forever now."

Ethan sighed with gloomy acceptance as he resolved to let go of any truth he thought he previously knew.

"If you're really him, and I believe you are, then I'll call you Mercury... Tell me everything I should know. And after that, tell me all the things you think I *shouldn't* know, as well," he requested. He'd grown weary of secrets.

Seventeen: Lovers & Kings — Secrets Revealed

NIGHT RULED OUR multiverse alone until Darkness stepped forward from the shadows. She was wild and beautiful, and it took little for her to win Night's heart. Together they bore triplets—two brothers and one sister—Somnus, the first Death, and Dawn.

Night split his kingdom into three realms and as a gift, once his children reached maturity, he gave them each dominion over one. Somnus would be King of the Dream World. Death, King of the Spirit World. Dawn, Queen of the Conscious World.

Feeling lonely, Somnus and Dawn each found lovers and had their own children. Death did not, for he was not lonely. He was surrounded by spirits and shared his confidences with his faithful comrade, Mercury, of whom he was very fond.

Dawn lost touch with her brothers, and due to her ever-growing family—each wishing to rule their own realms beneath her—found her powers stretched, her subjects scattered, and she began to lose control of her kingdom.

Somnus and Death paid her a visit one day to advise her in her governing of the Conscious World, but she was proud and did not like their meddling, so she turned away from them and cast them out. She pleaded to Night and Darkness to ban them from her realm, but her request was denied. To quell her anger, they instead minimized the scope of Somnus's and Death's influence over the Conscious World.

Tired of mediating squabbling, they moved to another multiverse, leaving the siblings to sort things out among themselves.

When Somnus's sons, Sandman, Nightmare, and Phantom, matured, he ordered them to infiltrate the Conscious World and intervene on his behalf to implement his will by causing mankind to know his desires for them.

Sandman, the one with the power to travel worlds freely, led his brothers to carry out their orders. Nightmare relished in this and gleefully enacted his father's bidding. Phantom was obedient for a time but eventually grew bored with his task. He was ambitious and began to see the possibility of something greater. He wanted to unite the realms as one again and believed he could rule the multiverse more effectively than all of them.

As the Guide of the multiverse, Sandman was instructed by Death to allow Mercury passage between worlds to deliver messages to all cosmic beings. The two became close as friends and over time, closer still as lovers.

This pairing displeased Phantom. He knew his brother was not playing with strategy, but the result would be the same. Sandman was already the favorite of Somnus and such an intimate alliance with Mercury would only cause him to win primary favor with Death as well. In other words, of the three brothers, it was Sandman who seemed set to inherit a throne.

In secrecy, Phantom betrayed his father and brothers to Dawn in the hopes she would kill them and appoint Phantom as the new King of the Dream World.

Dawn was clever and not easily fooled. She saw the hunger for power in Phantom's eyes and, behind them, viciousness and greed. She also saw the opportunity to have the multiverse reigned over as she saw fit. So she committed her own betrayal. She declared war on the other realms. Overpowering them and killing her brothers, she claimed victory.

Then she did something unexpected. She did not claim dominion over the defeated realms. Instead, she looked to the princes of Sleep. She saw compassion in Sandman and proclaimed him the new King of the Dream World. Death had no children but he did have Mercury and she saw fairness in him and proclaimed him the new King of the Spirit World. He would take the title of Death as he was so well known to those in her own realm as such. She appointed Nightmare the new Messenger and he was satisfied with the title.

Unsatisfied, though, was Phantom, whom she revealed as a traitor to his brothers. However, she was wise and turned him over to Sandman, the compassionate brother, to deal with as he saw fit. Sandman proclaimed Phantom an eternal prisoner of the Dream World and banished him to the shadows. Dawn returned to her own realm, pleased with her victory and confident in her choices.

Sandman and Mercury, lovers and kings, brought with their union harmony between their realms and balance with the Conscious World. As with most good things, this did not last long.

Phantom, shunned and filled with absolute hatred, haunted the Dream World as he watched every move Sandman made. He heard every word and observed every action, even the most intimate. In his maddened voyeurism, he found his key to freedom.

The carnal acts of passion he witnessed between Sandman and Mercury produced a miraculous side effect. A creation of energy. Not a cosmic being, as was born of celestial kings and queens, but a tangible essence of pure energy that flowed between the two as they transferred their passion. This energy would come to be known as Azoth—a quintessence of life force—immortality.

One evening, as Mercury passed through the veil of shadows separating their realms, Phantom quietly possessed the king's own shadow and lay in wait as Mercury went to greet Sandman.

Later that night, when Sandman and Mercury inevitably reveled in their passion, Phantom consumed the Azoth, bursting forth from the shadow, and stood on equal footing before them. He could now rival their power. In surprise, the two lovers released one another and the magic was dispelled for them but remained in the veins of Phantom as he absorbed it.

Phantom attacked Sandman and Mercury, in an attempt at murder, but Nightmare intervened. Nightmare was not immortal but had the ability to take the form of many creatures at once, so he confused Phantom, giving the lovers time to escape. But they did not leave. They knew what must be done. Phantom would never stop his quest for power until he was dead; and now, he could not die. Instead, they had to use the one advantage they had left over him, the gift of travel.

Sandman and Mercury, with Nightmare's help, transported Phantom to a faraway plane in the multiverse. So far away, in fact, Sandman feared losing his way, and so he forged the Sandman Orb, a spherical map of celestial power, to help guide himself back home.

They abandoned Phantom in this new world to spend the rest of eternity in solitude. A tragic mistake, for they had failed to realize this world harbored unknown demons, and he would be very far from alone.

Sandman, Mercury, and Nightmare returned home to find Darkness and Night waiting for them. Night had seen them traveling through time-space and assumed the worst had transpired in their absence. After hearing the tale from the kings and the prince, Darkness warned that Azoth would cause the destruction of their realms and their own demise, if any other beings ever learned of such powerful magic. Immortality must be banned and so, in turn, the cause.

Heartbroken, Sandman and Mercury agreed to leave each other, but Darkness knew what passion was and how tempted they would be with only a thin veil of shadow between them. She enlisted her daughter's help and Dawn was happy to oblige. Woefully, the lovers said their final goodbyes, and Darkness and Dawn took their spirits to the mortal plane and hid them each in the blood of different men to stay dormant indefinitely. In this way, their essence could survive, but they would not remember the other. Nightmare was tasked with hiding the Sandman Orb so no one would know the artifact's location. Darkness had thought to destroy the orb, but Dawn reminded her it held the key to Phantom's location.

Nightmare took over as King of the Dream World, and the title of Death fell to one of Darkness's younger children, Charon, who previously helped guide the spirits of the dead. There was an age of peace, so Darkness and Night, once again, took their leave.

And then an event happened so quickly its origin could not be traced. Somehow, Phantom made his mark in Dawn's realm. Demonic creatures, carrying a strain of tainted immortality, began to plague a world called Earth. The same world where Sandman and Mercury had been safely tucked away. These creatures earned a name. Vampire. Men began to show the ability to use cosmic powers. Magic. Then, they began to understand how to manipulate these powers to transform the world around them. Alchemy.

Rumor began to spread on the celestial planes. Phantom was back, and this time he had an army on his side. The Order of Azoth.

Eighteen: The Wrong Guy

"ETHAN, I FEEL I must caution you," Mercury stated as he gripped him supportively on the shoulder, after finishing the tale of their origins. "There isn't a single thing you can say in this moment that won't be incredibly cliché."

"Yeah, because being cliché is the thing I'm most concerned about." Ethan glanced at him incredulously. This was old news to him, but for Ethan, the universe had presented itself and unfolded with answers that led him to the worst possible conclusion. He'd opened his mind completely, and now even his own conscious reality was as surreal and hellacious as any other he could possibly dream up. In an annoying existential way, everything made perfect sense.

He had listened closely, and analytically, to everything Mercury told him. He had been shocked, embarrassed, and terrified. Now, however, his mind was keen to find an escape route, and if he'd ever been a champion at anything, it was embracing hope where others saw none. Also, loopholes. Most people in their early twenties knew how to navigate them well.

"So, Phantom—my brother—" The word felt weird to say. "—is out there in the multiverse somewhere, and somehow he's recruited followers: the Order of Azoth." Ethan's mind worked quickly. "And this *cult* is determined to hunt Travelers, but not to kill them. Because they need them?"

"Correct. You're a quick study." Mercury flashed a wide grin at Ethan's astuteness and willingness to accept the truth. "And at this juncture, 'them' is 'you.' They also need me, but good luck to the bastards with that. I live in the safe house."

"What?"

"The Spirit World," Mercury clarified, shaking his head slightly at his own cockiness. "I know I shouldn't act untouchable. They will find a way eventually, I'm sure. But for now, I do have comfort in the fact none of them can travel there. Not unless they're dead, and at that point, I'm no longer useful to them anyway."

"The Order can travel, has traveled," Ethan stated, mostly as a reminder to himself. "With the help of sandmen. Well, I'm never going to take any of them anywhere. I couldn't even if I wanted to. They're stuck on Earth forever now, so...crisis averted."

"Not so fast, moon child," Mercury readily corrected. "If you don't do what they demand by choice, then they'll command you with force. Also, they're well beyond Earth. Past Travelers, unfortunately, already spread them throughout the multiverse. There are sects all over the place. Earth is home to the largest now, but the most powerful division was once in the Neon Ghost Galaxy and wasn't anything to snub your nose at."

"The what?" The flood of names and places was pushing Ethan past the brink of whatever sense of sanity he might have left after Mercury's slapdash history lesson.

"The point is"—Mercury flitted his fingers as though his last comment wasn't worthy of explaining further—"you're outnumbered, love. And whether the impetus is Marcus, The Order, or nature itself, you will eventually figure out how to transport others at will, and we are all in danger."

Of course he would know about Marcus. Ethan realized, feeling a warm blush color his cheeks. He'd probably seen everything, either in real time or as soon as he'd looked into Ethan's eyes.

"If they ever succeed"—Mercury continued—"in capturing you and I both, then we're, and I emphasize this pun to its fullest potential, cosmically screwed. I'm already Mercury. They only need you to fully transmutate back into the Sandman, and then I'm sure you can guess what they'd try to force from there."

Ethan's face was revolted as he pieced their plan together.

"These aren't your traditional alchemists. They're enlightened to the true nature of the multiverse, and they seek a treasure far greater than gold. They seek true immortality. Controlling and having the sole claim over the source of Azoth would give Phantom a virtually indestructible army. He will attack with full force to overthrow the three realms and claim ultimate dominion over all. We *cannot* allow them to ever get that far because, Ethan, I honestly and truly do not think we'd win." He frowned.

Death had just spoken his death sentence. Difficult for Ethan to find any optimism in that. He stared silently at the alien grass beneath his feet which glowed and sparkled with stardust.

"Which leads me to why I'm here," Mercury segued carefully. "The spell you were working with Marcus—do you think you could recreate it on your own?"

Ethan looked to him suspiciously. "I don't know. I didn't get to finish, so I'm not even sure the spell worked."

"It was working," Mercury confirmed. "I need you to try again, Ethan. Alone. I want you to step through a portal from Earth to the Dream World, bringing your corporeal form entirely here. If you extract yourself from their reach and remain hidden, then we may be safe for a while longer."

"Why alone?" The question was the first that came to Ethan's mind. The whole point of learning to travel in such a way for him was solely for the purpose of being able to take Grady with him. He ascertained from Mercury's expression he expected him to leave everyone behind.

"Because once you're here, you cannot leave this place," Mercury stated firmly. "You'd be fine, but a human wouldn't be. Not for too long, anyway. There's nothing to sustain them. And being in hiding means staying hidden."

"I can't do that." Ethan shook his head in stern defiance. "I won't leave him. Especially if they're after me. They'll never stop. They'll kill him, trying to find me. I'm not a coward. I'd rather take my chances there with him than here with you. I know you loved him but—"

"Grady and I were very close but—" Mercury began to protest.

"No, not Grady. Sandman," Ethan clarified. "But I'm not him. You're wrong. You might be right in terms of everything else, but you're wrong about me. I'm not your celestial soulmate or whatever you want to call it. You've made a mistake."

There was no sadness in his tone. Nor any self-doubt in his words. Ethan sat upright, full of conviction, his eyes boring into Mercury's, begging him to read them.

"I see him every time I look at you," Mercury dismissed with a sad smile.

"Then look harder," Ethan pressed, his voice tight and sure. Mercury frowned with reservation, but he put his best efforts forward and stared deep, past Ethan's eyes, into his subconscious.

"I have traces of him in my blood, but his essence doesn't exist inside of me, does it?" Ethan asked. It was a leap of faith—a hunch. But listening to Mercury's story and remembering what Chris had taught him of the Sandman, as well, he was pretty sure he could do the math to this problem on his own. Who knew him better than himself, after all?

"Fuck me!" Mercury proclaimed. "How could this be!"

He flew off the bench and now he was the one pacing; his black cloak trailing behind his footsteps, kicking up clouds of dreams as he moved.

"So, I was right?" Relieved, Ethan felt renewed optimism.

"This isn't something to be proud of, darling!" Mercury pivoted to face him. His eyes combed Ethan's again, as though hoping he'd made a mistake. "I don't understand."

"I think I do," Ethan offered eagerly. "For once—"

"Oh? Suddenly an expert?" Mercury's expression was wild. "Do tell, poppet. We haven't got all day. You're still frozen in a high-speed chase with a Hunter, and if Sandy isn't here, then I have to found out where the hell he's gone off to!"

"You call him Sandy?" Ethan smiled, relishing in his brush of luck at not being some 'chosen one' figure after all. "That's cute. Dorky. But cute."

"We all have pet names," Mercury stated matter-of-factly. "Now please explain yourself. I have a celestial boyfriend who's apparently MIA, and I need to find him before *they* do."

"I don't know where he is," Ethan confessed. "But...you came right up to me. When I killed that vampire. How did you not see the truth in my eyes then?"

Mercury was momentarily quiet. Finally, he allowed a defeated sigh. "I suppose a small part of me suspected the possibility. But everything else was in your favor! I honestly hoped you would be him. Who else could he be? You're so goddamn adorable. I could've been entirely happy entangled in your lips for eternity."

"Um, yeah, okay." Ethan grimaced slightly. "So, basically what you're saying is you were willing to overlook the obvious because you're horny?"

"No, Ethan!" Mercury held his hand to his chest in feigned offense. Then he mulled the accusation over with fairness and shrugged, "I mean, maybe. Look, this doesn't make sense. You *have* to be him. The other Travelers are dead. That only leaves you."

He wasn't staring at Ethan anymore. His thoughts had wandered. Now he was staring directly over Ethan's shoulder at nothing in particular. Ethan glanced back to make sure no one else was there and then faced Mercury again.

"You can't track where he is?" Ethan prodded.

"No," Mercury admitted, breaking out of his small trance. "I've used my powers to try to hone in on him before. His spirit is truly missing."

"He's not in the Spirit World, is he?" Ethan pressed, feeling vindicated.

"You're not asking about Sandy, are you?" Mercury verified with a smirk.

"Sure I am." Ethan pursed his lips, accepting what he knew now to be the true state of things. "They're the same guy, aren't they? The Sandman and my dad."

"It would appear so," Mercury acquiesced. "And he's exceedingly adept at remaining hidden."

"All right, then." Ethan nodded slowly. "Got any bright ideas on how to find him?"

"A very bright one, in fact," Mercury confirmed. "Vincent was using the Sandman Orb the night he...disappeared. I have no idea where he is, but I do know where the Orb is."

"You do?" Ethan perked up at this. "Tell me. I'll go anywhere to get it."

"You won't have to go far," Mercury admitted. "Marcus has the Orb in his possession. Oh, and tell Grady to drink this." He handed over a vial filled with a deep crimson liquid.

Ethan was instantly suspicious.

"Don't worry. It isn't blood," Mercury reassured. "It is slightly bitter and little salty, though. But if I remember correctly, that never stopped Grady from swallowing before."

Ethan rolled his eyes; new identity, same old Dacey. His mind was too muddled with questions to let the remark phase him for too long. "Why does Marcus have the Orb? Did you two always know this? And how did you make a phone call from here? I can't even get cell service in Grady's garden half the time."

"I'm Death, darling. I'm allowed certain liberties to be as creepy as I'd like." Mercury flashed Dacey's famously charming grin. Then added as a matter-of-fact, "Also, the woman you nicked it from was a friend of mine. My number was already in her contact list. I simply exercised some supernatural power from there. Speaking of, there are a few incriminating photos of yours truly on her camera roll, and I'd be ever so grateful if you'd delete them before you give it back, or toss it, or whatever you decide to do."

Before Ethan asked him about Marcus's connection to the Orb again, or before he could inquire concerning anything else, Mercury rapidly strode toward him and placed his palm on Ethan's forehead.

"Now, go fetch," he instructed and broke through Ethan's time spell; waking him up.

ETHAN REGAINED CONSCIOUSNESS and time flowed back into a fluid motion. The side effects of the time spell sent a chaotic whirling net of psi energy, colliding with the Hunter who had been pursuing them.

Ethan looked on as the magical kinetic blow knocked the biker off course before he could pull the trigger. He'd lost control of his motorcycle, veering recklessly out of his lane. Before the bike flipped on its side, the Hunter leaped off and his body, which was still consumed in a light silvery and purple mist, went tumbling into a ditch while the bike skidded and wrecked into the back of a semi-truck. The truck driver immediately began to pull over.

Chris hit the gas and sped out of sight.

"I'm not sure what you just did back there," Chris shouted over his shoulder. "But I'm starting to appreciate your violent tendencies."

"I'm not violent. Just protective," Ethan corrected, turning to Grady to make sure he was all right.

"Whatever you want to call it, keep it up. You saved our asses," Chris said, taking a left onto a road that led to the outskirts of town. "I'm taking you both to Grady's, where you'll be safest for now. Then I'll go check on the others."

"What happened? Why do I feel so disoriented?" Grady immediately interrogated, sitting back up in his seat dizzily.

"I'll explain later," Ethan said, handing over the vial of liquid Mercury gave him. "Drink this."

"Where did you get this?" Grady took the potion in his palm and gave the concoction a quick inspection.

"A friend. Please, trust me," Ethan insisted. He saw Grady's house coming into sight, and he felt a small rush of relief to have a place where to, hopefully, regain his composure.

Grady trusted him after all. He gulped the dark liquid, grimaced at what must have been an unpleasant flavor, and pocketed the vial for further research.

Experimentally, he clenched and unclenched his fist. He seemed surprised, "It worked."

Chris pulled the car straight up to the front entry of the house and turned to face Grady, "Get inside. Run the lockdown protocol. I'll give you a call as soon as I'm with the others."

They both nodded, hopped out of the car, and headed into the large manor.

"Remind me to thank Chris for installing this security system," Grady said, punching a code into a small panel in the entryway. Ethan assumed there was a lot of technological magic involved because the perimeter of the house shimmered with the same silvery mist he'd seen quite a few times at this point.

"A healing potion." Grady glanced to him, bewildered. "Who gave it to you?"

"An old friend of my dad's." Ethan smirked. For once, he knew more than Grady.

Nineteen: Follow Him to Hell and Back

EVEN AFTER DOUBLE- and triple-checking the manor was secure, Grady still insisted they take up residence in a room without window access for the time being. Honestly, Ethan was impressed with the amount of work Grady and Chris had put in during his months away. Not only had they been diligently conducting espionage tactics and ambushes on the vampires who had flooded into the city, but they had also, effectively, transformed Grady's residence into a high-security magical fortress.

The signature violet and silver mist radiating on and along the perimeter of the property indicated ward spells had been employed. In this case, on a large scale. Grady explained they had spent weeks of Chris spellcasting and Grady performing rituals, connecting an intricate chain of various protection spells in the overall form of a pentacle that encased the manor at its center. The area was practically impenetrable, but they were dealing with the world's supreme mages; alchemists whose magical knowledge dated back to the ancients. They couldn't afford to be cocky. And so, away from windows and entrances, it was.

After a few minutes of anxious and adrenaline-fueled pacing, the two men eventually conceded that, until they heard back from Chris, the only option was to wait. Grady prodded Ethan again regarding the healing potion, claiming something that potent was beyond the scope of any normal witch or shaman. Ethan saw from the sharp glimmer in Grady's eyes he already suspected something similar enough to the truth. Ethan had met a celestial—a deity.

Ethan, still overwhelmed by the truth himself, threaded his fingers with Grady's and guided him to the Victorian-era, hunter-green couch. They sat beside each other, Grady assuming a casual, but vigilantly alert position, with Ethan facing him; one leg curled up half beneath him, knee lightly grazing Grady's leg. Ethan carefully, and excitedly, retold his entire encounter with Dacey. He did his best to remember every detail, although there had been so many, he wondered if he might have missed a few.

Grady was typically a man who took things in stride and rarely wore shock blatantly across his face. This instance was an exception. He appeared to sort through a wide range of emotions as his handsome face twisted and then rested again with each new bit of information. Ethan suspected he already knew half the truth. He'd been propositioned by the Order once upon a time, after all. He and Chris had already confessed that. Not to mention he'd learned a hefty bit in relation to Dream Travelers in the personal quest that had originally led him to Ethan's hometown. Their meeting hadn't been by chance, and Ethan secretly suspected he would never know the full extent of Grady's knowledge or experiences in regard to that, but he'd decided Grady's mysterious past was something he'd have to accept if he chose to trust him, and he did.

The part that appeared to genuinely surprise his enigmatic lover was the revelation that Dacey had been Mercury all along. Ethan didn't have to be a telepath to register the semi-smug look in Grady's eyes at the quiet realization he'd bedded not one, but two celestials in his lifetime. Ethan produced a wry smirk and slight eye roll but pushed onward, recounting the entire conversation. By this point, speaking the life-changing truth regarding his dad, Ethan became introspective, and his recap tapered off as he grew distant in his own ruminations.

FEELING AS SUFFICIENTLY caught up on things as possible, Grady scooped a comforting arm around Ethan's shoulders and pulled him in. Ethan leaned on him for support and rested his head on Grady's chest. Grady couldn't imagine what it must be like to go an entire lifetime thinking a parent was dead and then finding out they've been alive all along and are now within reach. Not only that, but they're a celestial king burdened with the power to destroy the world and people you love. Yeah, that didn't happen too often.

Grady lifted his hand from Ethan's shoulder to gently caress the loose tousles of black hair that lay across his forehead. He rested his cheek lightly on the top of Ethan's head and kissed him there.

"My cosmic prince," he whispered, full of admiration, compassion, and sadness. They both knew the truth now. There would never be a day when they weren't fighting for their lives. The universe was vast, the enemies plenty, and though they had his brilliance and resilience and Ethan's supernatural abilities, they were still—in the end—just two men against a multiverse seeking to destroy or enslave them. *Relationships. They're never easy.*

Suddenly, the self-doubt in terms of his mortal inadequacies dissipated. It didn't matter that he was human and flawed. All that mattered was Ethan chose to love *him,* and he loved him back with every bit of his unworthy being. He felt a fire ignite inside him. A rebellion within, against the odds of time and space, monsters, or evil alchemists. Nothing was going to stand in his way of spending the rest of his life, however short or long that may be, with the one person he loved most. He knew what must be done and he was determined to see they'd both survive. He couldn't imagine a greater purpose in life than protecting and loving a demigod.

"Right, then," he said. Grady lifted his head and cleared his throat. "I've met your mother. I suppose it's time you introduced me to dear old dad too."

Ethan sat upright, raising an eyebrow at Grady's bemused expression.

"You can't go with me," Ethan said. He looked uncomfortable trying to be assertive.

"I can and I will," Grady insisted, throwing his shoulders back with determined poise.

"I don't know how to travel with someone safely yet," Ethan reiterated, a slight edge to his voice. "I'm supernaturally impotent. Do you think there's a pill—or potion vial for that too?"

"Use that endless imagination of yours and figure it out. You're not going to go through this alone," Grady reassured.

"Right now, I only know one possible way." Ethan hesitated before continuing. His eyes seemed to search Grady's for a negative response. So Grady offered him a passive one. One he hoped said he'd decided to buckle himself in for this roller coaster no matter where things took them. He'd follow him to hell and back. Or in this case, the farthest reaches of the multiverse.

But all Grady actually said was, "Call him." He nodded, resting his elbow on the back of the couch as he leaned his head on his fist. His index finger lightly ran across the top of his lip as he became calculating. Marcus had the Orb; a fact he found highly suspect. "Invite him here."

"Do you even think he'll come?" Ethan pulled his phone out, confirming Grady's suspicion that he already had Marcus's number. He knew vampires far too well to expect anything less. They kept their prospects as easy to reach as possible. Ethan had him in his contact list within the first hour of their meeting; Grady was certain.

"For you? Yes. Just get straight to the point and hang up without explanation. Always maintain the upper hand when dealing with him," Grady advised wisely. "He'll come and he'll bring what we need with him. He won't be able to resist the bait. Sharks, too, can be reeled in."

Ethan kept his eyes trained on Grady's as he placed the call; no doubt to reassure him there were no secrets between himself and the vampire.

"Hey, I'm literally calling in a favor," Ethan said, indicating there had been an answer. He switched the phone to speaker so Grady could listen.

"I'm not generally a fan of favors." Marcus's voice quipped in return. "I prefer to generate debts. But, I suppose I can make an exception this once for a handsome doe-eyed boy. Tell me your needs, and I'll be happy to satisfy them."

He heard the flirtatious smirk in the vampire's voice. Grady's vision clouded slightly with jealously, but he kept silent.

"I want you to come to Grady's manor. I'm sure you remember the way from the Halloween party. Bring the book and the Sandman Orb. Text me when you get here," Ethan instructed.

"How do you know about—" Marcus began to ask, his voice cold and suspicious.

Ethan disconnected the call before he finished.

Grady produced his own phone and immediately dialed a number.

"Who are you calling?" Ethan asked.

"Backup," Grady answered simply. Then, in response to Ethan's inquisitive eyes, he said, "Another of your father's old friends. Suppose we do find Vincent? He has absolutely no reason to trust us. If he's not lost, then he's hiding and won't be happy to be found. We need to bring along a familiar face to mediate."

Ethan attempted a protest. "How many people do you expect me to take? I'm not a commercial airline."

Thankfully, Arthur answered before he had to respond.

"Arthur! Good evening," Grady greeted pleasantly. He extended an invitation for the professor to join them and only allowed a few vague details for the reason. He'd explain in full once everyone was together. After getting him to warily agree, Grady put his phone away.

He trained his attention on Ethan. "You look decidedly apprehensive."

Ethan frowned. "Just anxious about our lives resting on the back of my novice abilities."

Grady took both of Ethan's hands affectionately in his own and leaned forward to give him an encouraging kiss. He rested his forehead lightly against Ethan's so they were nose to nose.

"Don't worry. I have a plan," he reassured. The smile curving Ethan's lips now told him he trusted him. Which was good because Grady was ready to face things head-on. Together. As they had promised each other they always would.

Grady pressed his lips to Ethan's; their mouths parting slightly to feel the tip of each other's tongues. A rush of warmth overcame him as he tasted Ethan's kiss. Who knew when they'd have a chance to be alone together again? If the fate of the world and their friends wasn't enough of a motivator to succeed, then this definitely was. He wanted more of this. He needed more of this.

He'd do anything he needed to defeat the Order—for the good of the multiverse.

But mostly, for Ethan.

Twenty: The Collector

EVERYONE ARRIVED AT the manor without incident. It appeared the Hunters of the Order of Azoth had withdrawn while they prepped for whatever their next move might be. Grady, Ethan, and the others were under no delusions that the Order knew precisely where their target was located. They were either waiting for an opportunity to strike or the wards around the property really were worth their, metaphorical but also partly literal, salt in keeping the unwanted out.

Shortly after Grady contacted Dr. Arthur Ellis, Chris had returned with Karen, Edwin, and Benny in tow. Chris had expressed his wariness of the quiet frontlines. Nothing was registering on his surveillance monitors, when he'd stopped to review them, before packing up a few necessities from the office. No signs of the Order, no signs of vampires—nothing. Not even the local supernaturals, who were generally restless. He knew the Order must have tampered with his system, so he was hesitant to believe Grady's home security would be any less vulnerable.

Arthur hadn't taken long to show up and he was greeted with warm hugs from both Karen and Ethan

Everyone was in the study now, save for Marcus.

Grady filled everyone in on their situation as they waited but withheld the most vital bit of information— Ethan wasn't harboring the original Sandman within him.

They'd decided together that, for now, it was best no one else know who he really was, in case word somehow got back to the Order.

Suddenly, the door to the study swung wide open with Agatha, Grady's resident ghost maid, flying through above the intruder. She whirled her body around him, presumably incensed he'd barged into the manor without so much as a knock or ring of the doorbell.

Grady and the others stood, vigilant against attack at the disruptor, as he swatted the poltergeist out of his way.

"Marcus!" The name emitted from Grady's lips as more of an accusation than a greeting. "How did you get in?"

"You invited me," Marcus reminded him, lifting his nose pretentiously and glaring at Agatha as she dived back into the hallway. Once he was certain she was gone, he brushed his shoulders of any obtrusive ectoplasmic residue that might ruin the fabric of his cobalt Armani blazer.

"You only have to do it once," he added condescendingly, focusing on Grady and the group. "*Vampire.*"

"Yes, I know how *that* works." Grady clenched his fists in annoyance. Adding the blond daywalker to their band of misfits had already proved taxing, and he'd only just arrived. "How did you get past the wards?"

"Oh, those old things?" Marcus waved his hand dismissively and strode to stand by Ethan. "Please, Hunter. I've been breaking into supernatural institutions and houses of esoteric repute longer than you've existed on this tiny rock. I know how to pick a magical lock or two."

"Well, if he can get past them, then so can the Order of Azoth." Grady frowned at Chris, disappointed their security measures had been a failure after all.

"Those snake-oil space alchemists?" Marcus crinkled his nose with disapproval and he peaked an inquiring eyebrow. "What have they got to do with anything?"

"You know about the Order?" Ethan immediately interrogated.

In fact, all eyes in the room were now on Marcus. The vampire must have realized this because he straightened his shoulders to assert his dominance and scanned every face with his amber eyes like a lion evaluating its competition. If he deemed any of them worthy, his expression certainly didn't give anything away, and he retrained his attention on Ethan.

"I deal in black-market occult antiquities. You could say we have a history," Marcus revealed vaguely. "They know me as the Collector."

Ethan quickly met Grady's gaze.

"Ah, I see you've heard of me," Marcus mused, noticing their body language.

"You're the one the vampires are looking for," Ethan informed him.

"Well, that's...problematic," he stated flatly with a small grimace.

"What would they want with *you*?" Grady pushed, eager for answers.

"I suppose the same thing you do." Marcus shrugged as though he'd grown bored of the conversation already. However, he promptly reached into a brown leather satchel he'd brought with him, which hung over his shoulder, and pulled out a small shiny silver ball. He paused for a moment, as though considering if his next course of action would be the right one, and then handed the artifact to Ethan.

"The Sandman Orb." Chris's eyes lit up with reverence as he moved closer to get a better look.

"Where did you get that?" Grady asked, as though he'd ever trust the vampire's answer.

"Dacey didn't tell you during your pillow talk?" Marcus seemed caught off guard and Grady swore he saw relief dance across his features.

Reluctantly, Grady kept silent. Perhaps pillow talk was something he should have afforded Dacey because now it was clear important information being withheld.

"Well, 'where' is irrelevant." Marcus deflected in response to his telling silence. "You should be more concerned with 'why' I have it."

Grady corrected himself, "Fine. Why?" He mustered his patience as best he could. Grady watched as the Orb shimmered with blue and purple ripples of stardust in Ethan's hands. Ethan appeared mesmerized by the artifact.

"No, I wasn't offering a solution," Marcus clarified. "That's your riddle to solve. If I'd been interested, I would have puzzled it out ages ago. But I'd venture to guess the Order wanted to either prevent or ensure this exchange. I have no idea—nor do I care, honestly—which was their motivation."

Possibly noticing Grady was at his wit's end, Marcus generously offered more information, "A long time ago, a member of the Order brought this artifact to my attention. This, too, in fact."

He pulled out the codex and handed it over to Grady for perusing.

"First, he wanted the book for himself," Marcus continued, his expression harking back to a time long past. "And then, oddly, he insisted on giving the thing back. To Dacey, specifically. It was the strangest thing. I've always felt like he had a voice in his ear. Someone else pulling the strings. But, who knows? All alchemists seem inherently prone to insanity, and I haven't much patience for anyone with any belief structure founded so heavily in existential whimsy."

"Aren't they all?" As a scholar, Arthur couldn't help but add his two cents to the remark. Marcus offered a slight nod of approval at the jest.

"Well, now that we know Dacey is Mercury, that makes perfect sense," Chris spoke up. "The Sandman artifacts, Mercury... The only thing they would have needed to complete their trinity would've been a Traveler. If they controlled all three at once, then they'd have the ability to actualize their cosmic Manifest Destiny."

"*The* Traveler," Grady pointed out. Although, he didn't elaborate and the emphasis was lost on everyone around him except for its intended audience—Ethan.

"Dacey is what now?" Marcus obviously only held tight to the one fact he felt pertained to him.

"Mercury," Ethan answered. "He's alive...sort of. He found me. That's how I knew to ask you for this." He clutched the Orb tightly in his hands.

"He's very much still Dacey, but he's also Mercury. Essentially, he always had been. That's why his telepathic abilities were so strong," Ethan explained. "A god was in his blood the entire time. Now that I think of it, that might be why you were so enamored with him."

"A...god? Mercury...? Dacey is a god now." Marcus's lips drew into a prideful smirk. "Of course he is. I can't think of a role more fitting."

"Yes. But it's a problematic destiny," Ethan went on. "The abridged version is that by controlling Mercury, the Sandman, and these artifacts, the Order can wage a celestial war against reality as we know it, using immortality as their weapon of mass destruction."

"I deign to imagine the glorious Homer-esque poetry I'm missing with those Cliff's Notes, but I see now why you're alarmed," Marcus conceded a rare bit of sympathy. "I suppose that makes you a god, of sorts too?"

Ethan nodded, thankfully, unwilling to give away his secret.

"Figures. I've only ever been attracted to the most glorious of creatures." Marcus smiled primly and then promptly jumped into demands. "Bring him here. You promised. I've more than done my part."

"It's not that simple," Ethan began.

"I don't care what complexity level you deem it. The way I see things, you owe me a huge debt." Marcus's eyes narrowed with a steely flash of savagery as he glanced at the Sandman artifacts. Grady hoped Ethan was finally seeing the monster within.

"Really living up to that Collector nickname," Chris quipped. The joke was strained, however, as he was prepared for a fight.

"We don't have time for this." Grady chose to act reasonably. "Marcus, if you help us outrun the Order then you'll see Dacey anyway. The more bodies on our side, the better."

"This isn't my battle," Marcus argued.

"If you love Dacey then it is," Ethan stated with a calculated severity, sure to cut through Marcus's obstinacy. "You can be sure the Order will destroy every bit of him that may still exist in Mercury. Do you want to cower by and take that risk? Either you vow to stand by his side forever, or you choose to walk away now and never know him again."

It was a harsh hand to play, but Grady was proud of him. It was the truth, after all, and most likely the only argument that would sway him. Everyone in the room had already chosen to devote themselves to saving the Sandman and Mercury and doing everything in their power to stop the Order.

"Did he ask for me to commit myself to this?" Marcus asked Ethan softly. He must have still maintained hesitant hope that, after everything, Dacey still wanted him.

"Yes," Ethan answered limply. Grady knew he was lying; he was a terrible liar. "Yes. He asked for you to help us. To help *him*."

"If he requested this of me, then I will join your cause," Marcus agreed, buying into the fib, either out of true belief or eager desperation. "I've been captive to his whims since the moment I first laid eyes on him. I knew, eventually, he'd want me back."

"Right." Annoyed, Grady cleared his throat. "Then the first thing we need to do is—"

The sound of glass shattering permeated through the manor. Everyone in the room who wasn't already on their feet jumped to them again. Benny growled and attempted to run toward the doorway before Karen scooped him up.

The movement of intruders was easily heard; their attackers weren't afraid of confrontation.

Agatha, this time accompanied by her ghostly husband, John, glided back into the room in another full tizzy over what she presumed were more rude guests.

"These *weren't* invited. Do what you can to hold them off," Grady told the ghosts, asserting a minor cross gaze at Marcus.

The Order was easily heard bursting into rooms, searching for the inhabitants.

"I've never been in a fight before," Edwin chimed in as he grouped in closer to Arthur and Karen.

"Great. Super reassuring," Chris sighed. He swung a black bag he'd been carrying, off his shoulder and pulled out three small insect-like drones. Their surfaces were black and their mechanical wings shimmered with silvery magic. He waved a hand over them which activated his spellwork and they took off flying around the room, waiting for his command. He then retrieved a wristband, similar to the one Ethan had during their vampiric encounter at the furniture store, and strapped the device on.

"Well, I know you've used one of these before," Grady encouraged, handing Edwin a pistol that would normally seem a bit too antique for effectiveness, but he had firsthand knowledge the weapon still functioned suitably well.

"I could hold them back myself, or try a time flux, but I need to use my energy to open the portal and get us out of here," Ethan informed, a slight panic rising in his voice.

Marcus rested a hand on his shoulder. "Believe it or not, I've survived this kind of thing before. Focus on the portal; we'll handle the rest. Whatever you do, though, do *not* get distracted."

There wasn't time to question him. Ethan set to his task and began to draw in as much energy as quickly as possible.

Grady knew the energy drain was working because a flux occurred in Chris's equipment. It must have done so with the Order's, as well, because he heard them collectively making a fast descent on the study. They'd homed in on their target.

Twenty-One: Sacrifice

ETHAN STRUGGLED TO maintain his concentration while trying to open the portal, with pandemonium literally surrounding him. His friends had formed a semicircular shield of bodies to protect him, while he stood within proximity of the fireplace, the codex opened on a wooden side table. He'd hidden the Sandman Orb within his jacket; their destination didn't need to be traced. Thankfully, having performed the same exercise earlier in the evening, he easily recalled the details of the ritual. Unfortunately, there hadn't been time to construct the safety net of a protective transmutation circle as Marcus had done previously. He'd have to rely simply on skill, vigilance, and blind luck.

However, he kept defaulting to distraction. Precisely what Marcus had warned him *not* to do. It was difficult not to focus on the catastrophic noises breaking out from behind him. The people he loved most in the world were in that room, and they were putting their lives on the line to protect him. That singular truth became his incentive, forcing him to focus. He *had* to concentrate. He *had* to succeed. Anything less and they might not survive.

THE HUNTERS OF the Order of Azoth hadn't arrived alone. They'd brought along roughly a dozen of their willing vampire lackeys. Only four actual Hunters were present, and they were easily discerned from the group as they donned black jackets that wrapped around their hands to form fingerless gloves. The material resembled leather but was imbued with protection spells. Waves of shimmering silvery magic rolled across the surface as they moved, causing the illusion of a holographic sheen. Their pants and combat-style boots shared the effect and each outfit was covered in loops and buckles that held various weapons in place. Most had short, dark hair but their faces were hard to distinguish, as they each wore shades with green lenses actively broadcasting some sort of information to them. They were effectively indiscernible. Except for one.

A tall, slender man in his mid-thirties had strolled in behind the rest and took a lengthy drag off a questionable-looking cigarette. He was exceptionally different from the other Hunters. He sported well-groomed and meticulously styled, short, red hair. A splash of freckles adorned his features and grew denser near his pale-green eyes. His outfit of choice was also a far cry from the rest. He was dressed in a nicely form-tailored gray trench coat, complete with rather snug pinstripe dress pants, matching vest, black oxfords, tie, and black leather gloves. An eye-catching pin on his coat's lapel glistened—depicting a symbol of some sort—but they were all standing too far way to be able to tell what it was when he entered the room. Save for those such as Chris, who already knew the emblem well.

The man casually admired the room before flicking his vice to the rug beneath him and putting it out with the toe of his oxford.

"I appreciate a well-curated home," he complimented with a cold smirk.

"I sincerely doubt that," Grady remarked, narrowing his eyes crossly at the burn on the antique runner.

The man frowned and snapped his fingers as he instructed his men, "Engage and apprehend the target."

In mere moments, Grady's study transformed into a battlefield.

The vampires attacked first, determined to bring down those protecting Ethan as he continued to work on drawing in psi energy.

Marcus and Chris joined Grady, making for a quick defense as they were the most adept at combating vampires.

Chris sent his drones into action as they flew toward three vampires who had already singled out Karen as an easy target. One of them, however, seemed surprised to find she wasn't quite as helpless as she looked as she drove a stake into its torso with acute precision. Beginner's luck or not, the other two vampires were caught off guard by her swift defense, and the drones were able to take them out.

Seeing the potential for fast failure on their part if the drones finished off the rest of the vampires as easily, one of the Hunters immediately brought them down by emitting a cyberpathic interception link and fracturing Chris's connection. The Hunter reset the drones' targets on each other and let them demolish themselves.

"Shit!" Chris spat. Usually, the Order kept their techno-mages behind screens and in laboratories. Grady assumed they called one into the field precisely to counteract him. Which meant he hadn't been as "dead" to them as he had previously anticipated.

Grady, always a believer that the best defense is a good offense, immediately shot a dart of poison, collected from a Mongolian death worm, at the obnoxiously chic man who had dared to ruin his favorite baroque print rug. However, the shot was intercepted by another Hunter. Grady discerned they were under orders to the effect that protecting this well-dressed man's life was somehow a priority over capturing Ethan. Why? He had no clue, but it was an informational advantage he immediately mentally catalogued.

Benny, ever the loyal werehuahua, lunged at an attacking vampire and clamped his jaws on its ankle. This only vexed the creature but was enough to distract him as he stumbled around the room trying to shake the fierce little canine off his pant leg.

Arthur took advantage of the distraction Benny's bravery provided and slayed the creature with a Manananggal fighting spear he'd quickly ripped from one of the global oddity displays on the wall.

"Good boy!" Arthur congratulated. Benny barked an enthusiastic thanks and wagged his tail before taking off to hunt down another leg to offend.

Grady stole a glance to check on Ethan's progress. His body was pulsing with the influx of psi energy.

He held his palms out, his body radiating with a visibly blue aura, and emitted the energy as he began to rip open the veil between dimensions.

One of the vampires had made its way close enough to stage an attack on Ethan. Before Grady was able to shout a warning, Marcus whipped a fire iron out of the stand next to the fireplace and lunged the makeshift weapon into the torso of the young vampling, pinning him to the wall. While the wounded vampire tried to pull itself free, Agatha and John flew by and tossed a couple of Grady's wooden stakes to Marcus.

Marcus nodded a polite gesture of thanks to the poltergeists before they departed the room. Grady knew Ethan was funneling energy at an accelerated rate, and they most likely didn't want to risk being pulled in.

As two more vampires lunged for Ethan, Marcus, faster and more experienced in combat, easily staked one through the heart with his right hand while he tripped the other with his left foot and then quickly knelt to stake him effortlessly through the back. Grady hardly believed his own eyes. Marcus had valiantly—and without hesitation—saved Ethan.

"They certainly don't make us like they used to." Marcus frowned at the fallen vampires.

Seeing the portal was already opening, and their small vampire army had been less than effective against the sandman's friends, the Hunters became ruthless. One pointed a small, sleek, black handgun, with pulsing neon green stripes conforming to its shape, aiming at Chris. As he pulled the trigger and released a vibrant green ray of lethal energy, Chris pressed a small button on the side of his wristband and maneuvered the underside of his arm out to block him. A net of precast spellwork shot out and formed a mystic shield, absorbing the Hunter's shot. The device caught the energy like a Venus flytrap and snapped back to contain it within the safety of the wristband compartment.

Taking the offensive, Chris sprinted forward and tackled the man to the ground. He didn't need the assistance of witchcraft to pummel his fists into the Hunter's face. The strange ocular device the man had been wearing flew off as Chris railed on him. The Hunter grappled for a dagger attached to his belt with one hand while he used the other to try to stave off the oncoming blows.

Before he could intervene to help Chris, Grady was flung backward into a bookshelf and collapsed to the floor with the force of the hit. Gloved hands grabbed him by his collar and hoist him up into a now-disheveled collection of classic gothic literature. Caught off guard, Grady resorted to grasping a heavy bronze bookend and swinging the blunt object upside the head of his aggressor. Thankfully, the Hunter hadn't anticipated the blow, and the knock to his temple rendered him either unconscious, or dead; Grady hadn't the time or compassion to assess. He tossed the man to the side and rejoined the fray.

Karen and Edwin had sought shelter behind the Victorian chaise lounge, but two of the vampires spotted them and moved quickly for them.

"Karen, look out!" Grady shouted. Thankfully, Karen was alerted, but unfortunately, this outburst caught the attention of another passing vampire, who then spun on his heel to lunge at Grady.

Frantic, Karen spotted one of Grady's revolving handheld crossbows still sitting on his weapons table. She ran to grab it and spinning around, took aim and sent a stake flying into the neck of one of the vampires. Edwin scrambled out of the way, as she took a second shaky shot, this time landing a stake through its heart. Watching the other go down, the second vampire halted his attack, but his indecision gave Karen enough time to discharge another stake and end him.

"Have you used one of those before?" Edwin remarked with a stunned but relieved grin.

"Nope. First time," Karen admitted with a proud smile, "I guess the Roam family are just fast learners."

"They certainly are," Edwin responded, his gaze now on the phenomenal sight of Ethan's powers.

SURPRISED BY HIS own strength, Ethan had widened the portal to the Dream World by a five-foot radius. The laws of nature were fighting back, though, and maintaining the gateway's stability grew more difficult. His arms began to shake as they buckled under the pressure of resistance. His head pounded and a piercing pain was beginning to shoot through his skull from the back of his brain to his eye sockets. He kept pushing himself harder, despite the difficulty.

THE DAPPER MAN commanding the attack narrowed his eyes as he watched Ethan work his magic. He didn't seem to regard him in the same awestruck manner as the others in the room when they turned to assess his progress. His eyes gave away he'd seen similar powers before. Instead, he looked calculating.

"Fetch!" Arthur instructed Benny. The little dog dutifully ran toward one of the remaining vampires and leaped onto his pants, clamping his jaws on his crotch. The vampire shouted obscenities in shock, and Arthur, once more, used the dog's distracting maneuvers to his advantage by staking the vampire's heart through from behind.

One of the vampires locked his sights on Karen as she and Edwin were distracted by the magnificent sight of Ethan's portal. Chris positioned himself carefully and initiated the one-use gamma ray on his wristband. A flood of excruciatingly bright light poured out and disintegrated the vampire on the spot.

"I'm completely useless to you all. I never should have come here," Edwin confessed to Karen as they realized their near brush with death.

"Don't be ridiculous," Karen reassured as they both backed up closer to where Ethan stood to help hold the line of defense. "I know Grady's guarded, but trust me, you've given him some much-needed closure."

They watched as Grady stood over the last vampire from the Hunter's small army and used his khukuri knives to slice its head off with the morbidly swift grace of a professional killer.

"I'm afraid closure is a gift my son will never possess," Edwin stated grimly as Grady turned to face them. Their gazes met and he saw the sorrowful cold truth. Grady had not lied to him; he hadn't uttered empty words of self-denigrating melancholy. His son, Alexander Quinn, had died many years ago. The man who stood before him now may have his face, but his eyes confessed the similarities ended there. He may have found love again, but for him, there would be no peace. He was caught in another war aside from the one they all faced. He was locked in a crusade against himself. He'd joined the realm of monsters, and his harrowed soul would never rest.

ONLY TWO HUNTERS remained standing, and one was the man in the suit. They glanced at each other, and then, sharing some silent cue, both pulled out the same peculiar guns the other Hunter had used and began shooting chaotically amidst the group.

"Now!" Ethan commanded. He'd managed to stabilize the portal, but he wasn't sure how long he'd be able to hold the gateway open. The shots firing around him echoed like he was underwater as the pressure building inside his head from the psi energy only increased. He was beginning to see dark spots in his vision.

Benny, small and agile enough to zip through the chaos around him was the first to run past Ethan and hop through the portal.

Chris was shot in the side as he attempted to shield Karen and Edwin from the line of fire. His body crumpled to the floor as he grabbed at his wound in writhing agony.

"Chris!" Karen tried to run to his side but was stopped as Arthur reached out and grabbed her arm. Shots were still being fired, and he wasn't going to let her run to her death.

"Go! Please!" Chris urged her as he lay immobile on the hardwood floor.

Karen, her eyes brimming with tears, allowed Arthur to take her by the hand and pull her to safety through the portal.

Chris let his head fall back against the ground with a soft thump.

Determined to leave no man behind, Grady leaped to Chris's aid, but the Hunter who had shot him was on them in an instant. He and Grady grappled over Chris's body.

This distraction left Ethan exposed. Marcus was the only thing standing between him and the man in the suit.

"Allow me to help you join your brethren in eternal hellfire," the man said as he pulled another gun, loaded with a silver and wooden bullet, from his coat and fired a sure shot point blank at Marcus who had no way of defending himself in the moment. Moving off mark would only put Ethan on the receiving end of the bullet, and no matter what it was made of, a bullet was still a bullet.

Courageously, Edwin dove in front of the vampire, taking the hit.

His body buckled beneath him, and he fell lifelessly before Marcus's feet.

Marcus and the Hunter both appraised each other with surprise, momentarily astonished by Edwin's selfless sacrifice.

Grady had laid an effectively disabling punch to the other Hunter's nose which had sent the man stumbling backward.

"No!" he cried out in desperate disbelief as he caught the tail end of his father's brave actions.

The lead Hunter was unrelenting. His deadly one-shot weapon now empty, he tossed it aside and pulled out his handgun again. He moved in swift bold steps toward them as, this time, he aimed at Grady, who appeared frozen in the midst of an internal struggle.

"I can't hold it!" Ethan warned as the edges of the portal began to flux.

Marcus ran to seize Grady around the waist and dragged him into the portal against his will.

The Hunter switched targets to Ethan, about to pull the trigger.

Ethan jumped through behind Marcus and Grady and closed the portal before the bullet even left the barrel.

"FUCK!" THE HUNTER, Chase West, shouted in anger and kicked over a small table. A heavy book fell to his feet with a thud.

He lifted his leg to kick the tome across the room, too, until he realized what offending object was. A stroke of luck. A consolation prize.

He wiped a gloved knuckle across the top of his lips as he regained composure and then knelt to retrieve the tome.

Grasping the book, he stood again and surveyed the damaged, the dead, and the wounded.

He pressed the small gold pin on his lapel and a shimmer of magic waved across the "☿" symbol it formed.

"Report," the disembodied voice of an older man rang from the pin authoritatively.

"Failure. Subject escaped," Chase replied. "However, I've gained control of the codex. And I have a prisoner who might prove useful." he eyed Chris, who was still cringing in immense pain on the ground.

"Thank you, Chase. Not what I had hoped to hear but not an entire waste of time. They've only delayed the inevitable," the voice responded with resigned acceptance.

"Will you alert the High Council, Lord Vid?" Chase asked, pushing rank to even question.

"Mr. West, I *am* the High Council," Vid corrected, with a cold snap, before adding, "Initiate the Infiltration Stratagem."

The transmission was disconnected.

"Asshole," Chase murmured, this time lighting up a joint as the only other remaining Hunter hoisted Chris's injured body over his shoulder.

Twenty-Two: In Dreams

THE DREAM WORLD gleamed vibrantly with its rich perpetual hues of purple twilight. Stars flew, zigzagging above them, at an accelerated and seemingly unnatural speed. The setting would have been tranquil and beautiful had it not been filled with heartrending cries of despair.

"Ethan! Wake up! Please, wake up!" Grady was on his knees, surrounded by the soft blue shimmering grass of the Dream World. Each blade danced with effervescent stardust.

He wrapped his arms tightly around Ethan's unconscious body, clinging desperately to him, and pulling him close against his chest.

The others had gathered around Karen, who was also on the ground holding her son's arm, checking for a pulse. She and Grady's tears both flowed freely.

Ethan had succeeded. He'd brought them to the Dream World—most of them, anyway. But the amount of energy he'd had to use to accomplish the feat had proved immensely taxing on both his mind and body.

Everyone was hovering over him, hoping he'd survive.

"*Please*! I love you. Wake up! *Come home, Ethan*," Grady pleaded again, desperately using the words they'd once designed as an anchor to pull him back from unconsciousness. Distraught tears rolled down his cheeks as he held onto Ethan's unmoving form and kissed his temple with despair. "You can't leave me too. Not you."

The words were muffled and garbled in the wetness of sorrow-soaked skin between his lips and Ethan's cheek.

"Oh, good grief. He's not dead, if that's what you're worried about," a cloaked figure said, approaching. The man removed his hood. "Trust me. I'd be the first to know."

Startled, Grady and the others looked to see who'd sauntered up beside them. Marcus's eyes widened in fascinated surprise.

Benny let out a short odd yip, which is when everyone seemed to notice he was no longer a dog, but very human and inconveniently naked.

"Oh, allow me to help," Mercury offered, appraising his nude form with a mischievous smirk. He considerately took off his cloak and tossed it to Benny. "I'm afraid this is all I have to offer, but you'll find the breeze beneath quite pleasant, I can assure you."

"Thanks?" Uncertain gratitude was all Benny seemed able to manage at the moment.

Mercury caught Marcus's gaze, and he smiled warmly. "You're as handsome as ever." He embraced Marcus openly.

"Everything he said about you is true," Marcus assessed after they hugged and shared an affectionate kiss in greeting. He looked Mercury over, clearly impressed by Dacey's new status.

"That I outrank all of you now? Yes. Quite true." Mercury smirked coyly and tapped Marcus fondly on the tip of his nose. He might have ventured to steal another kiss if Grady hadn't taken the opportunity to knock Marcus off his feet with an unexpected right hook to the side of his face. Marcus stumbled, before tripping and falling onto his bottom.

Grady loomed above him, fists and jaw clenched in fury.

"Darling! Now is not the time for crimes of passion," Mercury attempted to jest. He promptly grabbed Grady by the arms to stop him from attacking Marcus again.

Marcus brushed his hands against his own cheek as he hoisted himself from the ground and found blood was smeared across his fingertips. His eyes grew wild with astonishment.

"I'm bleeding," he stated stupidly.

"Yes, my love," Mercury confirmed. "The Dream World can alter cursed states a bit erratically. You'll fluctuate between vampire and human form. As Benny may from dog to human. Quite inconvenient. I told Ethan to come alone but true to sandman form, he disregarded sound advice."

"You killed him!" Grady bellowed at Marcus, not caring one bit whether he was facing a vampire or a man. He attempted to wrestle free from Mercury's firm grip. "You killed my father!"

"Like hell, I did!" Marcus spat back and shoved Grady's chest.

Mercury had to crowbar his celestial body between the two and, exasperated, sent out a mild pulse of magic into both men's chests, knocking them off their feet and back to the ground, separate from one another.

"Do gather your wits, gentlemen!" Mercury ordered. "Your behavior is most unbecoming and more aptly— unhelpful."

"My father would still be alive if it weren't for that egomaniacal piece of shit!" Grady yelled, glaring daggers at Marcus.

"Oh, go fuck yourself, *Hunter*! Might I remind you, you'd be dead right now if it weren't for me," Marcus shouted back with a callous scoff and dismissive roll of his eyes. "So, don't blame *me* for *your* daddy issues!"

"*Don't* say my name like that," Grady growled in defense. "Don't you dare equate me to them! I am *nothing* like the Order!"

"You are *exactly* like them!" Marcus let out a small coldhearted, incredulous laugh. "No, I take that back. You're *worse*! At least the Order doesn't live a life of false pretext. You've conducted yourself as they do, but you won't admit the truth. Not to yourself or the people who are stupid enough to trust you! I bet they never even would have found Ethan if you hadn't imposed yourself into his life and forced him to use his abilities. That's all you really are, Grady. An imposition to everyone who's known you. You're a fraud and a murderer. And you're going to get everyone killed!"

"Enough!" Mercury bellowed. His voice resounded through the Dream World with a booming authoritative echo only a deity could summon. Everyone grew silent.

"Really, is this what you've devolved to?" Mercury frowned at them both with disapproval. Marcus opened his mouth to respond, but Mercury interrupted. "Hold your tongue! Dear heart, I love you endlessly, but you can be a real prick sometimes. He just lost his father. Go easy on him."

Mercury faced Grady. "I know you're inclined to wallow in contempt and self-pity, but those human privileges will have to wait. Marcus isn't at fault for your father's death and neither are you. No one is to blame but him. He died to save Ethan. He made that choice. All of you did. A possible fate you accepted simply by coming here."

Grady and Marcus mustered their self-control and slowly stood in deference to Mercury. He chose to avoid eye contact with Marcus. Instead, he turned his attention back to Ethan, who was now being held, mildly alert, in Karen's arms as she spoke soft encouraging words to rouse him from his unconscious state. When he looked back, Grady saw Marcus frowning in disgust as he vehemently brushed off his pant legs.

"He'll be all right?" Grady sought confirmation of Ethan's condition from Mercury in an attempt to let his feud with Marcus go. At least for the time being.

"He's fine!" Mercury grinned enthusiastically. "He's a Dream Traveler. He'll perform far more challenging miracles before his time is up. He simply pushed himself a bit too hard, considering his inexperience. He's home now, though, so he'll find his recovery a speedy one. And thank goodness for that because we'll need him to do it again soon."

"You can't be serious?" Arthur frowned, glancing up from Karen's side where he'd moved to give his support. "You expect him to do it again?"

"And again and again and *again,*" Mercury reiterated with an erotic lilt of seduction in his voice. "You'll find he'll build up the stamina for such things rather easily. Everyone's first time is usually their worst."

Ethan's eyes slowly began to flutter with awareness.

"Aha! See. I knew he'd rejoin us shortly." Mercury tilted his chin with delight. Then he looked to Grady and Marcus again, "You brought the Orb and Codex along, I hope? Hand them over, please, darlings. I need to help lover boy set his course."

"He has the Orb, but he didn't bring the Codex. There wasn't time." Marcus revealed, a frown of annoyance flickering over his features.

"Oh, fuck me!" Mercury sighed but shook his head with only mild disappointment. "No matter. He's got the gist of things, so while the journey may be rockier, he should still be able to reach Vincent."

"What!" Marcus's revived mortal complexion reverted back to being white as a ghost, or in this case—a vampire.

"What do you mean—reach Vincent?" Karen asked carefully, sharing a hopeful, expression with Arthur.

"He didn't tell you?" Mercury faltered, raising an inquisitive eyebrow.

"He told me," Grady answered truthfully, his voice low. He purposefully avoided the betrayed gazes he knew he'd be receiving from Karen and Arthur. He rested a hand on one hip and raised the other to rub the tension building on the bridge of his nose between his eyes. They all had reasons not to trust one another, but somehow, they still had to remain a united team.

"Are you saying Vincent...my husband is still alive? You know this as a fact?" Karen asked, almost breathlessly.

"Yes, darling," Mercury answered. He glanced in Marcus's direction. "Quite so."

"I have to find him. And bring him here," Ethan chimed in, having regained his wits as he sat up on his own.

"Why in the devil would you suggest such a thing?" Marcus demanded. He approached Mercury until they were merely inches apart and placed his hand upon his wrist in what appeared to be a silent plea. "You can't put Ethan at risk like that. He's safe here. Away from the alchemists."

"Love, we both know that's not the risk you're concerned about me taking," Mercury replied in a sharp whisper, which Grady was close enough to hear, staring him down pointedly. Whatever he meant, the remark caused Marcus to revert to his preferred form of protest. Silence.

Mercury went on to add to the others. "He must do this quickly. We're in a race against time now. Vincent is the true Sandman, not Ethan. Existence, everything you know, everything you love, everyone you hold dear is on the brink of being destroyed. We have to retrieve Vincent before the Order learns the truth; assuming they haven't already. Until then, no one—nothing—is safe."

VIVIAN EDWARDS, GRADY'S former secretary, bolted upright in bed in a panic. She had broken out into a cold sweat that had her short, black, bobbed hair plastered onto her cheeks, and her heart was still pounding against her chest. She took a few calming breaths as she recovered from her disorienting nightmares. She had grown used to morbid dreams after having her mind hijacked by another witch months before, but this nightmare was an entirely different experience.

She glanced at the alarm clock by their bed before shaking her boyfriend, Thomas Strong, who was snoring next to her, awake. It was 3:33 a.m.

"What the...what's going on?" Thomas blubbered as he was roused from a deep sleep.

"Grady and Ethan," Vivian said as she tossed back the sheets and turned on the light in the small apartment bedroom. She almost tripped over one of the yet-to-be-unpacked boxes near the bed as she scrambled to the dresser to grab some clothes.

"What?" Confused, Thomas sat up and rubbed his eyes, adjusting them to the sudden brightness.

"I had a dream," she explained. Then quickly modified that. "A premonition. They're in trouble."

"It's Grady. When *isn't* he in trouble?" Thomas moaned in annoyance as he began to slump back onto the bed. She knew his opinions on Grady hadn't changed. That had kind of been the whole point of skipping town to start a new life.

"I'm serious, Thomas." Vivian scowled and snapped her fingers at him to get out of bed. "I think I know where they are. We have to find a way to communicate with them."

"Slow down, sweetheart." Thomas got out of bed and walked over to face her. He rubbed his hands across her arms in a soothing caress. "What *exactly* did you see?"

"Death," she answered, fear gripping her voice. Her body was trembling. She looked fearfully into his eyes. "He set a trap... I saw how everyone dies."

About the Author

Vampire apologist and lifelong enthusiast of classic gothic horror, cryptids, and the occult; Dez Schwartz writes Dreampunk & Paranormal LGBTQ Fiction with a spellbinding balance of darkness and humor. When she's not busy writing, she can most likely be found with a latte in hand, perusing antique shops for oddities and peculiar vintage books or wrangling her demonic (but adorable) cats.

Email: dezschwartzauthor@gmail.com

Facebook: www.facebook.com/DezSchwartz

Twitter: @dez_schwartz

Website: www.dezschwartz.com

Other books by this author

Roam

Also Available from NineStar Press

Connect with NineStar Press

www.ninestarpress.com

www.facebook.com/ninestarpress

www.facebook.com/groups/NineStarNiche

www.twitter.com/ninestarpress

www.tumblr.com/blog/ninestarpress